THE CRYING GIRL

Other mysteries by Glen Ebisch:

A Rocky Road
Unwanted Inheritance

AVALON romances by Glen Ebisch:

To Breathe Again
Woven Hearts

THE CRYING GIRL

•

Glen Ebisch

AVALON BOOKS
NEW YORK

Published by Thomas Bouregy & Co., Inc.
160 Madison Avenue, New York, NY 10016

Library of Congress Cataloging-in-Publication Data

Ebisch, Glen Albert, 1946–
    The crying girl / Glen Ebisch.
        p. cm.
    ISBN 978-0-8034-9829-7 (hardcover: acid-free paper)
    I. Title.

PS3605.B57C79 2007
813'.6—dc22

                                        2006101347

PRINTED IN THE UNITED STATES OF AMERICA
ON ACID-FREE PAPER
BY HADDON CRAFTSMEN, BLOOMSBURG, PENNSYLVANIA

91.502

Prologue

Hazel Wilmot stood in the hallway of the old inn, listening intently. She'd waited long enough. If she had to do this by herself, so be it. An open door was an invitation to investigate. Although her eyes weren't all they might be at seventy, her ears, she assured herself, were just fine. At first she heard nothing, but then she thought that in the distance, somewhere in the back of the building, there just might be a sound. The sound of someone crying. Turning on a large flashlight, Hazel reached in the pocket of her nylon windbreaker and touched the revolver just to be certain that it was still there, then she headed down the central hall toward where she knew the kitchen was.

These people were very clever, she thought with grudging admiration: nothing too obvious, just enough of an enticement to lure someone who was already looking to venture into the house. The light moving from window to window upstairs had been faint enough to make one wonder whether it was real or some kind of odd reflection of the moon off the antique glass. And the crying that now

1

grew louder with each step she took managed to convey an almost otherworldly anguish while remaining muffled and uncertain.

The door at the end of the central hall stuck slightly, but with a solid shove it pushed inward on its creaky hinges. The beam of her flashlight showed a large farm-style kitchen extending along the entire back of the inn. A battered table, which probably once served as a combination preparation and staff eating area, filled the center of the room. The large sink along the back wall still had a hand pump standing over it like a silent guard, but Hazel suspected that it served at most as a backup source of water. The inn, after all, had been in use in the 1950s, she reminded herself, so somewhere along the way indoor plumbing must have been installed. Whether it functioned after years of abandonment was another matter. The same could be said for the dusty, out-of-date appliances that lined the opposite wall, bulky but silent without working electricity.

The sobbing was closer now, coming from the far end of the room. A door in the corner was ajar, and a faint glimmer of yellowish light led her on like a lighthouse beacon. She slowly crossed the kitchen, the wide boards creaking loudly with every step.

Reaching the door, she took the revolver out of her pocket with her right hand and held it directly in front of her. She stretched out her left arm and cautiously pushed the door with the end of her long flashlight. It swung open with exceptional ease, as if someone had oiled it recently. She took a tentative step forward. Her flashlight revealed a long wooden stairway leading down into the musty-smelling depths of the original basement. She saw that the stairs ended at a hard-packed dirt-and-stone floor. The flickering light was coming from somewhere in the back of the basement, and as she stood there determining what to do, the sobbing suddenly grew in volume and became even more heartfelt.

Hazel played her flashlight carefully down the stairs. On one side was a wall that seemed to be a deteriorating mix of earth and stone; on the other, where a railing should have been, there was nothing except an open space to the floor below. There were no risers between the stairs. Shining her light between the steps revealed little except what seemed to be an old wooden stepladder set up under the stairs, as if someone has been about to begin repairs then thought better of it.

Being careful to stay to the wall side of the stairs, she took one careful step, bouncing slightly to evaluate the soundness off the wood. It seemed to offer solid support, so she slowly descended one more step. On the next step, she told herself, she'd be able to bend down below the level of the floorboards and shine her light around the basement to see what awaited her.

As she was about to take the next step, the crying stopped. Hazel paused, unsure whether she should rush down the stairs before the cryer escaped. Deciding not to be hurried into doing anything that could be dangerous, she carefully extended her foot toward the next step. Just as she touched the wooden stair, hands reached up from between the risers, seizing her left ankle in a firm grip. Instantly she could picture someone standing on the ladder under the stairway and pulling on her foot.

Desperately she tried to step backward to the safety of the step above. Her sneaker came off as she tried to slip away, but the hands held firmly onto her ankle, continuing to pull her forward and off balance. She dropped the revolver and clawed at the dirt wall, desperate for something to hang onto, but it crumbled away into useless dust. Finally she twisted to her left, reaching out for a railing that she knew wasn't there. Then, with a cry of anger and frustration, she plunged off the stairs and toward the hard floor.

Chapter One

The double window in front of her desk looked out across the wetlands and above the row of toylike houses along the beach to a strip of azure ocean that still held the last hints of a dramatic, early-October sunrise. Her job as senior editor at *Roaming New England* magazine didn't pay a lot, Amanda Vickers thought, as she gazed out the window, but it did provide her with a million-dollar view.

Situated at the top of a small hill right off of Route 1 in Wells, Maine, the old house that served as the offices of *Roaming New England* was a bit dilapidated. However, despite its noisy plumbing and a cranky heating system, it occupied a much-sought-after piece of real estate, which the owner of the magazine had so far refused to sell despite good offers from developers.

Normally Amanda didn't spend her first few minutes in the office on Monday mornings looking out the window. Priding herself on being organized, she would normally start the day by listening to her voicemail, thumbing through the paper mail—immediately discarding the junk—and turning on her computer to check e-mail. But on this Monday morning, her attention refused to focus on the work at hand. She knew the reason. Jeff was getting serious.

They had spent much of Sunday together in Portland where Jeff lived and worked as a lawyer, and she could sense that he wanted more from her than the two dates a month they'd shared since last May. He hadn't said anything, but she could tell that he was mystified by her insistence that she had to spend every other weekend down in Boston with her mother. She could understand his puzzlement. After all, her mother wasn't sick. Plus, she had two attentive sons residing a short drive away.

Whenever she opened her mouth to explain things to Jeff, however, the tightness in her throat made her decide to wait until a better time. But she knew that if she wanted to hang onto him, the moment was rapidly approaching when she would have to be honest or risk losing him.

"Morning," Marcie Ducasse, the assistant editor, said cheerily as she bounced into the chair next to Amanda's desk.

Her curly red hair and full face glowed with health and good spirits. Short and sturdy, she was looking particularly colorful in a kelly-green sweater and a pair of tan chinos. Amanda, a few inches taller and slender, with straight blond hair, knew that in her tailored ecru blouse and dark-brown skirt they were a study in contrast. She took a deep breath and managed a faint smile. "Good morning."

Marcie frowned. "Not feeling well this morning?"

"I feel fine."

"A little too much of a good time with Jeff over the weekend?" Marcie asked with a mischievous smile.

"We had a good time," Amanda replied blandly, not anxious to encourage an exchange of confidences.

Although Marcie was twenty-two, only six years younger than herself, Amanda had a hard time seeing her as more than a child. Partly that was because she was right out of college, hired only four weeks ago. However that wasn't the full reason why Amanda couldn't think of her more as an equal. It was also a matter of the difference in their personalities.

There was something cheerfully naïve about Marcie, a willingness to happily believe everything she was told until she learned otherwise; whereas Amanda saw herself as a skeptic, someone who believed nothing unless the sources had been double and triple checked. Maybe it was because of her background in journalism, or perhaps it was a more fundamental difference in attitude. Either way, Amanda knew that it had created a small but significant gap between them.

"I'm almost done editing that story on the Portuguese fishing families of Provincetown," Marcie said, taking the hint and putting on a more businesslike expression.

"That isn't scheduled until December."

"I know. But we seem to be pretty well caught up right at the moment, so I figured that I'd get a little ahead."

Amanda nodded. Whatever Marcie's personal traits, she was an accurate and efficient editor. When Amanda had started at *Roaming New England* two years ago, it had only been in existence for three months. Greg Sheffield, the managing editor, had put out the first three issues on his own. Amanda never knew how he had accomplished it. Even for two people it had been a strain to handle all the editing and layout responsibilities. Aside from visiting her mother, most of Amanda's waking hours had been given

over to the constant struggle to meet the deadlines necessary to get out the next edition of *Roaming New England*.
When Greg had finally convinced the magazine's owner
to hire an assistant editor, Amanda had breathed a deep
sigh of relief. She reminded herself now that she should
show her appreciation of Marcie's contributions.

"I've been meaning to tell you," Amanda said, putting
a smile on her face, "you've been doing a great job the last
month."

Marcie smiled back. "Oh, you say that to me every
week, not that I ever get tired of hearing it. I love working here. I can't believe that I was lucky enough to get a
job doing what I enjoy right out of college. And I'm learning so much."

Amanda nodded. "That is the advantage of working on
a small publication." She didn't go on to add that the dis-
advantages were an equally small salary and not much
room for advancement. Why discourage the girl, especially when she was both willing and needed?

Since Marcie looked like she might be ready to launch
into a lengthy description of the joys of working for the
magazine, Amanda quickly tapped in the code for her
voicemail and put it on speakerphone. Neither Jeff nor her
mother ever used the office line, so she wasn't concerned
that Marcie would overhear a personal message. The first
two calls were from freelance authors: one wondering
about payment, and the other objecting to some cutting
Marcie had done on his article about catching bluefish off
of Cape Cod.

When the third message began, Amanda wondered
whether she shouldn't have listened in more privacy.

"Hello, Amanda," a strong but older woman's voice

said. "This is Hazel Wilmot. When you sent me that note in your Christmas card two years ago telling me that you were working for *Roaming New England*, I bought a subscription just to see what one of my better former students was up to. Although I have enjoyed the magazine in general, especially the historical articles, I was a bit surprised to see that you have begun writing a column called 'Weird Happenings.' As you might imagine, I don't approve of spreading stories about ghosties and ghoulies; however, your tone of polite doubt is encouraging. At any rate, I may have a story for you from right here in Shadsborough. Apparently people are hearing a girl's voice crying at night in the cellar of the abandoned Shadsborough Inn. Rather a common ghost story, I know, but perhaps I can find a new wrinkle in it for you. Call me when you get a chance." A phone numbered followed.

The call had come on Friday, right after she had left early to see Jeff. Amanda frowned, annoyed that two days had passed already. She didn't like to seem inefficient, especially to Hazel Wilmot.

"*Who* was that?" Marcie asked when Amanda stopped the next message from beginning.

"Professor Wilmot. She was one of my biology professors back in college."

"I thought you majored in English?"

"I double majored."

"Wow! English and biology." Marcie rolled her eyes. "How did you ever do that in four years?"

"Went summers and took overloads," Amanda replied vaguely, her mind preoccupied with the message.

"And you still hear from your professors?"

"She was my advisor, so I saw a lot of her."

"She must have liked you if she stays in touch."

Amanda shrugged. She'd never been quite sure where she stood with Professor Wilmot.

"I worked hard and got good grades. She liked that. But Professor Wilmot wasn't the warm and fuzzy type. I think she was always disappointed that I didn't go on to graduate school in biology."

"But you write to her?"

"Yeah. I started after graduation. Once a year at Christmas I send her a card with a note inside updating her on what I'm doing. She writes back with a succinct summary of the past year's events." Amanda paused for a moment. "I guess I starting writing to her because even though she could be kind of stiff, I think she really cared for me in her own way. Plus, she was the kind of person whose respect you wanted to earn. If I wasn't going to become a scientist, I figured that maybe I could still impress her with my growing journalistic career."

Amanda smiled to show that she was half joking.

"Where is Shadsborough, anyway?" Marcie asked.

"Somewhere in the middle of New Hampshire."

"So are you going to call her back and find out what this haunted inn story is all about?"

Amanda glanced at Marcie and almost couldn't keep from shaking her head. The eagerness to hear about another outlandish event was written all over the younger woman's face. Amanda had repeatedly tried to instill some degree of skepticism in Marcie for the supernatural tales that were sent in to the magazine for the "Weird Happenings" column. Marcie, however, was still inclined to take each one at face value, more interested in the excitement it produced than in its truth.

Granted, it wasn't the job of the magazine's staff to

investigate each report to see if it was a genuine supernatural phenomenon; they simply published the stories after checking with the author to make sure that the events had been described accurately. Explanations were left to the reader's imagination. Still, Amanda's scientific side kept her from believing anything improbable that she hadn't actually observed for herself. This wasn't the case with Marcie.

"I probably will call back," Amanda replied with forced casualness. "But right now I've got some budget figures to check over. Want to help?" She reached in the center drawer of her desk and took out a thick sheaf of spreadsheets.

"I guess I'd better get back to my office," Marcie said quickly, hopping up from the chair. She made no secret of the fact that she wasn't a numbers person. In fact, she often said that the sight of too many of them in one place made her break out in a rash. "Is it all right if I e-mail that fisherman who was complaining to you about the way I cut his story?"

Amanda nodded. "But don't let him worry you too much. A writer is always unhappy, even if only one word of his precious prose is cut."

"Yeah. And how many times can you hear about him hauling in another helpless fish without it getting repetitious?" Marcie paused in the doorway. "You'll let me know what this Professor Wilmot's story is all about when you find out?"

"Will do."

Amanda heard Marcie's heavy tread go down the hall to her office at the front of the second floor of the old house. She picked up the phone and tapped in Hazel Wilmot's number. A man's voice answered with a gruff "Hello."

"May I speak with Hazel Wilmot please?" Amanda said.

"Who is this?" the man demanded.

Amanda coolly stated her name. She knew that Professor Wilmot had been widowed for over twenty years. Who could this abrupt man be?

"And what are you calling Mrs. Wilmot about?"

"I'd prefer to discuss that with her."

"You can't."

"Why not?" Amanda snapped.

The voice on the other end paused for a moment, then went on a bit more gently, "Because she's dead."

Chapter Two

"Dead?" Amanda knew that she'd heard the man correctly, but a part of her mind wanted it to be a mistake.

"That's right. Now do you mind telling me the purpose of your call?"

Only half aware of her words, Amanda explained the message on her machine. Only when that was done did her reporter's instincts slowly return.

"And who are you?" she asked.

"I'm Tyler Hudson, Chief of Police in Shadsborough."

"How did Professor Wilmot die?"

There was a pause on the other end of the line as if the chief were taking the time to carefully think out his answer before delivering it. When it came, his response was disappointingly brief.

"She fell down the cellar steps of the old Shadsborough Inn."

Amanda stopped breathing, then consciously forced her lungs to fill with air.

"When did this happen?"

"We figure it was sometime on Saturday night."

"How do you know?"

Another long pause followed, as if the chief were debating whether to answer. "On Sunday, her next door neighbor brought her the newspaper. When no one answered the door, she came inside and found a note on the kitchen table from Hazel dated Saturday. It said that she was going to look around the inn that night. If we didn't have that note, I don't know when we'd have found her body."

Hazel Wilmot had called her late in the afternoon on Friday. Not getting an answer, she had decided to investigate the inn on her own the next night. *Maybe if I'd been here, she wouldn't have gone alone. Then she'd still be alive,* Amanda thought, feeling a familiar headache start behind her eyes.

She forced her mind back to the present. "What about this crying in the cellar of the inn that she told me about in her message? What's the story on that?"

The chief sighed wearily. "Every small town in New England has at least one haunted house. There's always a few folks in town who want to make it out to be more than it is."

"Professor Wilmot wasn't that kind of person," Amanda snapped. "Has there been a recent event that would have drawn her attention?"

Another pause, even longer this time. "Did you say you were some kind of reporter?"

"I'm an editor. *Roaming New England* is a regional magazine."

"Yeah, well, I guess you've got the whole story, then. What's your number there?"

Amanda recited her number. Before she could ask any

more questions, Chief Hudson had given her a quick word of thanks and hung up.

She sat back in her chair and looked out at the ocean, trying to calm down enough to think through what she had just learned. After a few minutes, her breathing had returned to normal and her thoughts were under control enough to evaluate the evidence.

Hazel Wilmot was a hard-nosed skeptic of the first order, but Amanda also knew that like most scientists she also could be intensely curious. If she heard about a ghost sobbing in an old house, her first assumption would be that either people were imagining the whole thing or someone was down there actually crying. Naturally that would lead her to want to investigate.

Another thing that Amanda knew about Professor Wilmot was that she had a streak of self-confidence bordering on arrogance. Some students had found this trait annoying. Others thought it gave Professor Wilmot a more human side. At any rate, Amanda knew that the professor would be absolutely fearless because she always figured that her own abilities would get her through any situation. Amanda could easily imagine her marching into a so-called haunted house in the dark of night when the average person would turn tail and run the other way; what she found harder to imagine was that Professor Wilmot had fallen accidentally down the stairs.

The professor might have been stubborn and a bit cocky, but she was never careless. Amanda could still picture her in the lab laying out all the equipment in advance and thinking through the entire experiment before taking the first step. Professor Wilmot was a small wiry woman who always seemed to be in complete control of herself and everything around her. However, even careful people get older, Amanda reminded herself, and become weaker and less agile, increasing the possibility of having an accident. But in her last letter, written only six months ago, Hazel had said that she was still skiing downhill and traveling to a gym in Concord three times a week: not the typical behavior of a fragile senior citizen.

But even fit, careful people can have accidents, Amanda thought, playing devil's advocate to her own suspicions. It was still a possibility to be sure, but not a clear certainty. And if Hazel hadn't fallen by accident, then what *had* happened? The word *murder* went through Amanda's mind like a banner headline. *Don't jump to conclusions*, she warned herself, there's no solid evidence to support that idea. Still, why had Hazel, a woman who believed there was nothing that couldn't be explained scientifically, suddenly become so interested in a ghost story? Could that have gotten her involved in something dangerous? Knowing the answer to those questions suddenly seemed like a driving need.

The quick shuffle she'd received from the chief of police didn't give Amanda much confidence that he was committed to digging very deeply into Professor Wilmot's death. He seemed more than happy to settle on an accident as the cause. But then he may not have known Hazel all that well, or, Amanda thought less charitably, he might be lazy, inexperienced, or unwilling to rile things up in a sleepy small town. *If only I had been here when she called*, Amanda thought again, feeling a new wave of guilt surge up inside of her. She remembered the therapist telling her after her father's death that guilt was a useless emotion, that instead of wallowing in it she should use her guilt to produce something positive.

That's what I'll do, Amanda decided, suddenly resolute. *Instead of sitting here feeling guilty, I'll try my best to find out how Professor Wilmot died.*

A half-hour of planning later, Amanda walked across the hall and into Greg Sheffield's office. Intent on editing an article, he didn't glance up. One of the many things that Amanda admired about Greg was his ability to focus completely on whatever he was doing. She wondered if he had always been able to put all his energy into the project at hand, or whether his early years as an overseas reporter had taught him to work under any conditions, ignoring discomfort and distractions.

Maybe it was this discipline that made her think of him as so much older than his thirty-five years. Or it could have been his full head of prematurely white hair. In any event, he certainly had an approach to things that made him seem more mature than most men his age. For the two years that they had put out *Roaming New England* almost single-handedly, she had never seen the pressure get to him. He always remained even-tempered and organized. Although Amanda knew almost nothing about his private life except that he was involved in a long-standing relationship with a woman who worked in Boston, she thought of him as a good colleague and a friend.

She cleared her throat. Greg glanced up and took off the half-glasses he used to read. He held the manuscript in one hand, as if weighing it.

"Another Monday morning and another article on a little-known but decisive skirmish of the Revolutionary War fought in a New England village. Sometimes I wonder whether people make these stories up. Do you think we could be publishing a whole new genre: historical fiction that claims to be fact?"

Amanda shrugged. "I know that we required the author to provide a list of his sources. Beyond that there isn't much we can do. We're not an academic journal."

"I know, we're in the business of entertainment."

Amanda paused, not sure how to proceed with what she wanted to say.

Greg watched her for a moment and realized that she had something serious on her mind. He gestured to the chair next to his desk. "Would you like to sit down and talk about it?"

She nodded gratefully and took a seat.

"I'd like to have a few days off to investigate a story," she blurted out, always a great believer in getting directly to the point when asking a favor.

"Investigate?"

"It's a potential story for '*Weird Happenings.*'"

Amanda stopped, waiting for Greg to object. But he skipped right to the heart of the matter.

"Since you know that the magazine doesn't attempt to investigate the truth of those stories, there must be something here that makes this situation unique."

She nodded and went on to explain the message from Hazel Wilmot and her conversation with the chief of police. When she was done, Greg nodded.

"I can understand why you'd feel bad about not getting her message promptly. Although you have to remind yourself that even if you had spoken to her, she might still have gone to the inn on Saturday night to investigate. From what you tell me, in addition to being a fearless and determined woman, she probably liked to go her own way."

"Somehow, knowing that doesn't make me feel much better."

"And there's really no reason to believe that this whole thing was anything more than a tragic accident. A dilapidated house can be a dangerous place in the dark."

"I'm sure Professor Wilmot was capable."

"All the same, one loose step or broken board and a person could take a fatal fall. It might happen to anyone."

Amanda didn't say anything. Greg seemed to sense that she was just barely tolerating his attempts to make her feel better because he went on quickly. "On the other hand, I can see why you don't have complete confidence in this Chief Hudson to look into all aspects of the accident. We don't know what the situation in Shadsborough, New Hampshire, might be, and given your personal relationship with Hazel Wilmot, I can understand why you want to make sure that all avenues are explored."

"Does that mean you'll let me go?" Amanda said.

"What's the status of our next two issues?"

Amanda quickly explained that they were actually further ahead than they ever had been since she had worked for *Roaming New England*. She was careful to attribute a large part of the new efficiency to having Marcie on board.

"So she's really helping out?"

"Definitely."

"No problems?"

Amanda hesitated a moment.

"Aside from her incessant enthusiasm and inflated optimism, I mean," Greg added dryly.

Amanda smiled. "She's young."

"And not a hard-bitten journalist type like the two of us."

"And probably never will be. She's not going to learn investigative reporting at *Roaming New England Magazine*."

Greg was silent for a long moment. "Maybe she should."

"What do you mean?"

"I know this '*Weird Happenings*' column we started a year ago is our most popular feature, but it worries me. You've seen the e-mail and the letters we've been getting from every nutcase in the Northeast, folks who think their houses are haunted, their neighbors are witches, and their woods are filled with spirits from the next world. We're starting to attract a real cult following here, and I'm not sure I like it. If we're going to publish this stuff, I think we have some responsibility to make sure that it isn't completely fabricated."

"A lot of the stuff comes from reputable people who gather folk tales and local stories. We even have some people with scientific backgrounds in parapsychology and extrasensory perception who write for us."

"But what about those stories that come from unprofessional sources? Shouldn't we either reject these articles or at least make some attempt to check them out?"

Amanda sat back in her chair. What had begun as a simple request on her part was developing into a complete turnaround in magazine policy. "You've never mentioned these concerns before," she said carefully.

"Not because I haven't had them, but because there was no way that the two of us could get out the magazine and at the same time check on this material. Now maybe we can accomplish that. We started this column as a way of keeping the magazine afloat, so we could publish more worthwhile material on the ecology and history of New England. I think it's time that we tried to exercise some control over these paranormal stories. We're both skeptics, so that shouldn't be hard."

"But you want *Marcie* to go out in the field with me to investigate these supposed happenings?" Amanda said. She didn't dare shout because Marcie was right down the hall, but she certainly wanted to. "Marcie loves this spooky kind of thing. She'll believe whatever the locals tell her, the more horrifying the better. She has no experience in sifting out the truth from the fairy tales."

Greg leaned back in his chair and smiled. "You might be underestimating her. After all, someone once trained me to be a journalist, and somebody on the *Boston Globe* trained you about eight years ago. Maybe it's time for us to give something back to the profession by training Marcie."

"I'm not sure she's got the personality for it."

"We won't know until we try."

"You mean until *I* try."

"You are her boss. Think of it as mentoring."

Amanda stared at Greg, thinking that in addition to being mature, he could also on occasion be maddening. Finally she raised a hand in a gesture of surrender. "Okay, as soon as I get back from Shadsborough I'll start training her."

Greg shook his head. "You know as well as I do that the best way to learn is to go out in the field and just do it. Since everything around here is so nicely up to date, I should be able to handle the shop by myself for a few days. Why don't you and Marcie go to Shadsborough together and find out what happened? How about you leave tomorrow and come back by Friday afternoon at the latest for our weekly review meeting? That will give you almost four days if you need them."

Four days of Marcie's bubbling enthusiasm might be as much of a trial as investigating a sudden death, Amanda thought. But Greg was a reasonable boss, and she knew that there was no point in arguing over whether she had to take Marcie along. He'd clearly made up his mind, and he wouldn't budge since it was part of a larger editorial decision with regard to how the stories for "Weird Happenings" would be handled.

"Okay," Amanda said, barely able to keep her feelings from showing on her face.

"I know you're thinking that Marcie might be more trouble than she's worth," Greg said in an understanding tone. "But remember, someone felt that way about both of us at one time. And, who knows? She might turn out to be surprisingly helpful. At least she's cheerful."

"Yeah," Amanda said grimly. "There is that."

"And check in with me once a day while you're out there."

Amanda raised a quizzical eyebrow.

"I want to know if you're onto something really good or not. We might have to bump something from next month's issue if this is a really hot story."

Amanda nodded. She thanked him and left the office.

As Greg watched Amanda leave, his own expression turned somber. Homicide or accident, he wasn't about to let Amanda go alone into the middle of New Hampshire investigating this death without support. Marcie might not be much, but right now she was all that he could spare. And checking in regularly would help. Whether it would be enough, he wasn't sure.

Chapter Three

Amanda opened the hatch of her green Subaru. Marcie took her bag out of the trunk of her small sedan and put it in the back next to Amanda's. They had decided to start out from the magazine parking lot because they'd be coming back there for the staff meeting Friday afternoon.

"It's a great day for a drive," Marcie said, looking out over the wetlands to the ocean with a wistful expression, as if not sure whether she'd ever see them again.

The breeze off the ocean blew her curly hair back from her head into a reddish halo, and she shivered. Amanda wondered whether Marcie was going to prove to be the right person for this job. Yesterday she had taken the news of Hazel Wilmot's death with a mixture of shock and fascination, readily agreeing to go to Shadsborough. Today, however, there seemed to be an undercurrent of reluctance.

"How about you be navigator?" Amanda said, handing Marcie the unfolded map once they were seated in the car. "I looked over the route last night. Shadsborough is near the White Mountains, north of Concord. I think we'd do best if we go down and catch Route 4 out of Portsmouth to U.S. 93, then head straight up." Amanda traced the directions with her finger.

"I guess it will take a while," Marcie said, frowning.

"I figure about three hours. There's no direct route between here and there."

"Sure looks like an out-of-the-way spot." Marcie's usually cheerful voice sounded a bit doubtful.

"Yeah, we were lucky to get a place to stay right in town," Amanda said as they pulled out onto Route 1 and began to head south.

"I suppose if it's in Shadsborough, it's not at a Hilton or a Sheraton," Marcie said.

"The Lost Trail Inn. A bed-and-breakfast."

Marcie stared at her. "For real? I thought B&Bs always had happy names like Dappled Oaks or Peaceful Pond."

"Not in Shadsborough, I guess. But the good thing is that the place is on the same street where Professor Wilmot lived, and when I talked to Pat Bennett, the woman who runs the inn, she told me that Hazel was a good friend of hers. In fact, she was the one who found the note saying that Professor Wilmot was going to the inn Saturday night."

"Maybe she can tell us more about what's been going on in town."

Amanda nodded. "Since the police chief doesn't seem to be very helpful, we'll have to try to depend on local contacts to fill us in."

"What reason did you give Pat Bennett for our visit?"

"Pretty much the truth. I told her about Hazel's call and said that I felt some responsibility to look into what happened for personal reasons. She seemed to accept that."

"Did you mention that we worked for a magazine?"

"No. I didn't want to make her nervous thinking that we'd put her every word down in print. If we do decide to write a story about this, then we'll tell her who we really are and conduct a proper interview."

"Do you really think we'll be able get a good story out of this?" asked Marcie.

Amanda's face hardened. "I'm not really concerned with whether we get a story. I want to find out the truth about what happened to Professor Wilmot. If that turns out to be something we can write about, fine. If not, I'll still be happy just knowing what happened."

Marcie nodded and remained silent.

"Sorry," Amanda said a moment later, "that came out stronger than I intended. I guess this is kind of personal for me."

"I understand. It's just that Greg told me that we might be doing more of this kind of investigative stuff, so I figured that he wanted us to get a story."

"Yeah. But this one is special." She gave Marcie a relenting smile. "Of course if we get a really neat story about a haunted inn, that would be icing on the cake."

Marcie nodded. "Greg said you'd teach me about investigating. All I really know is how to edit stories that are already written, I've never really done any reporting."

"You'll find it's not really that hard. You ask people questions, then listen carefully to what they tell you and even more carefully to what they're trying not to tell you. The hardest thing is learning to take notes on the spot that you can use."

Marcie nodded but continued to look uncertain. "You learned all of this stuff when you worked for the *Boston Globe*, right?"

Amanda nodded.

"That's a pretty good newspaper, isn't it?"

Amanda said that it was and suppressed a smile at the innocence of Marcie's question.

"So I've been wondering . . ."

"Wondering what?"

"Well, I like working on *Roaming New England,* but it's not exactly a major publication. Wasn't it kind of a comedown to leave the *Globe* to work on the magazine? Why did you do it?"

Amanda kept her eyes on the road. There was no way she was going to tell Marcie about the night she had broken her promise to have dinner with her father and only arrived in time to see the EMTs carrying his body from the burning house. If she had been there when she had promised instead of working late on a story, he would never have fallen asleep on the sofa with a cigarette in his hand while waiting up for her. That was the story that she'd never found the words to tell Jeff. Only Greg knew. She'd had to tell him in order to prove that she was serious about working at the magazine and not using it as a quick stepping stone to another newspaper job.

"The hours were too long. I couldn't have any life of my own. That's the way it is in big-city journalism."

Marcie eyed her doubtfully. "Still, you must miss it."

"Everything is a trade-off," Amanda said in a tone that suggested the topic was closed.

Aside from comments about the sights along the way and giving directions, they didn't say much for the next couple of hours. By then they were about ten miles from Concord, where they would take the interstate north. Amanda had noticed that Marcie's silence seemed to be mixed with apprehensive glances out the window, watching the heavily forested sides of the road as if expecting something to jump out at them.

"Looking for signs of deer or moose?" Amanda finally asked.

Marcie managed a weak grin. "I don't like to admit it, but I guess I'm a little claustrophobic."

"Being in the car makes you nervous?"

She shook her head. "It's being surrounded by all these woods. I grew up out west. My dad was career Army, and when I was a kid we were always stationed somewhere out there, either on the plains or in the Southwest. So I could always pretty much see to the horizon. That's why I like living by the ocean. It's open, and you can always see where the water meets the sky."

"But most of New England is like this," Amanda said, nodding toward the forest that fell like a heavy green curtain drawn along the sides of the road.

"I *know*," Marcie said, irritated for the first time that Amanda had known her. "Don't worry, I'll adjust. When you grow up an Army brat moving from place to place, you pretty much learn how to adjust to things."

She thrust her chin out defiantly, and for a moment Amanda could see the little girl going off for the first day in yet another new school determined to fit in by being friendly and upbeat.

I guess we all have our own demons, Amanda thought as she turned off for the exit to Route 93.

An hour later they stopped for a quick lunch at a fast-food place, then got back on the highway. A few miles further on, they left the interstate and turned onto the secondary road that led to Shadsborough. The two-lane road skirted along the base of a mountain that Marcie couldn't identify from the map.

At times the mountain was so close that it shaded the road from the afternoon sun, looming over them like a dark, massive presence. On the other side of the road was a forest of tall, straight pines that seemed to invite you to walk in among them and appreciate their cathedral-like height. But Amanda knew that anyone who was seduced into strolling very far might quickly find herself hopelessly lost after sunset in a maze of seemingly identical trees. She glanced over several times at Marcie, whose eyes stared straight down the road, focused on the only unobstructed view. Amanda considered giving her a word of support but decided that it might be best not to make any further comment on Marcie's problem.

Finally the pines on the left gave way to pastureland and a building came into sight, a dilapidated barn whose roof had long ago collapsed. It stood forlornly in the middle of what might once have been a carefully tended field but was now an overgrown meadow. Amanda wondered what had happened to the farmhouse and the farmer. Every abandoned building had a story behind it. In New England it was usually the story of a family that had struggled to eke out a living from the rocky soil, perhaps even succeeding for a while until eventually, either due to death or bankruptcy, nature had a chance to reassert its grip on the land. In another ten years, Amanda thought, you would be able to drive by the spot and not even know that a family had spent a lifetime attempting to make something out of this field.

A mile further along was an abandoned gas station that featured three rusted pumps standing at attention. An OPEN sign still hung in the window as if the last owners hadn't been able to face the inevitable. Amanda patted herself on the back for having the foresight to fill up the car before they left the interstate.

"Are we ever going to reach this town?" Marcie asked.

"Soon," Amanda reassured her. "Those were the appetizers."

Five minutes later, around a turn in the road, a sign announced the Village of Shadsborough. The road suddenly widened, and they came upon several colonial-style houses with white picket fences. This was quickly followed by a post office, a general store, a church on a tiny green, and a couple of more recently constructed public buildings, one of them labeled POLICE STATION.

The entire village was huddled at the base of the mountain, as if depending on it for protection. But even on a beautiful fall day like this one, the mountain seemed to Amanda to be more ominous than friendly, casting its dark shadow like a scar across the center of town.

"We make a left here," Marcie said as they approached a cross street.

Amanda put on the brakes and turned to head down the road away from the mountain. Unconsciously, she breathed a sigh of relief at putting it behind her. A sign hung from a white post on the fourth house from the left, *Lost Trail Bed and Breakfast*. She turned into a gravel driveway that crunched under the tires of her car as she pulled up to the front door. The inn was a rambling, white structure that extended back in several additions that clearly had been tacked on without any attempt at architectural consistency.

"This is it," Amanda announced, turning off the engine.

The two women sat there for a moment staring through the windshield at the building as though by common consent taking a moment to prepare themselves for what was to come.

"Ready?" Amanda asked.

"As I'll ever be," Marcie replied in a tone of grim resignation.

Amanda looked over at her and smiled. She was starting to like this new and less exuberant Marcie.

"By the way, who are we supposed to be?" Marcie asked.

Amanda gave her a puzzled look.

"Well, if we can't mention working on the magazine together, exactly what is our relationship?"

"How about friends and co-workers?" A mischievous thought occurred to her. "If anyone asks, let's say that we work as secretaries at an accounting firm. That sounds unexciting enough to prevent people from asking questions about our jobs."

"Accounting. Ugh!" Marcie said in mock disgust.

When they got out of the car, Amanda saw Marcie glance back over her shoulder apprehensively at the mountain that hovered a few blocks away.

"Does it make you feel closed in?" Amanda asked.

Marcie nodded. "This whole village has a place-that-time-forgot atmosphere about it. I don't know how folks live here all year long."

"Ask them how they do it when you talk to them. I'm sure they'll be happy to tell you all the details. One thing folks in small towns like to do is tell the outsiders how tough life is."

"Hello there," a voice called out.

Amanda turned and saw a tall broad-shouldered woman wearing a knit sweater and corduroy pants coming down the walk toward them.

"I'm Pat Bennett," the woman said, giving Amanda and Marcie firm handshakes.

Her gray hair was pulled back into a ponytail that served to accentuate her high cheekbones and good bone structure. Although she was clearly past middle age and wearing no makeup, Amanda noted that she would always be an attractive woman.

"How was your trip?"

"Long," Marcie said.

Pat laughed. "I know. You can't get from the coast of Maine to here without taking the scenic route. Your rooms are all ready for you. You're lucky. If you'd come last weekend, there'd only have been one room free so you'd have had to share."

"You were almost full up for the weekend?" Marcie asked, the amazement obvious in her voice.

Pat Bennett nodded. "I know we're a bit off the beaten track, but lots of city folks are willing to travel to come up here in foliage season. We're not quite at the peak yet. Two weeks from now will be even busier."

Amanda and Marcie took their bags from the car and made their way up the stone walk. The center hall of the house was darker and a bit smaller than Amanda expected.

"This is the oldest part of the house," Pat explained as if reading her mind. "It was built around 1810 and it's a bit more primitive than the two additions."

"When were they done?" asked Amanda.

"The first section was added on the back in 1870. The last section, which is really just the kitchen and sun porch area downstairs, was put on in 1925."

She led them up the stairs. Once on the second floor they went toward the back of the house, passing two rather dark bedrooms. The floor slanted upward somewhat disconcertingly as they went from the older portion of the house to the new.

"Here you are," their hostess said, stopping in front of two open doors across the hall from each other. "These are part of the 1870 addition, so they're larger and a bit brighter. The bathroom is at the end of the hall. You have this floor all to yourself. My husband and I sleep downstairs. When you're settled in why don't you come down to the kitchen, and we can have a chat?"

Marcie walked into the room on the right and glanced out the window. "Do you mind taking this one?" she asked Amanda.

Amanda saw the mountain framed in the window and nodded her agreement. Marcie smiled and went across the hall.

Fifteen minutes later, when she was done unpacking, Amanda surveyed the room. A four-poster bed covered with a quilt and a profusion of flowery pillows filled the center of the space. The inside wall was taken up by a large dresser with a curved mirror on top. On the side of the room toward the window was a bedside table on the top of which was an ornate gas lamp that had been electrified. A small writing desk and a chair were in front of the window. Almost every flat surface was covered with vases, seashells, small statuettes, and other knick-knacks. Although not to her taste at all, Amanda could appreciate that a lot of effort had gone into decorating the room in a country style typical of a hundred years ago, which evoked the atmosphere that people who came to a New England B&B expected.

Amanda stood by the writing desk and stared out the window at the mountainside. Although it was only late afternoon, the sun was half hidden by the top of the mountain and fingerlike shadows extended across the lawn on the north side of the inn. The center of town would already be in partial darkness, Amanda thought, and she shivered at how long and cold the nights would be in winter.

Maybe Jeff was right, and this trip had been a mistake. Her call to him last night explaining why she would be out of town for a few days had been a difficult one. Although he didn't come right out and say it, she could tell that he didn't understand why Amanda felt such a sense of responsibility to someone she hadn't seen in almost a decade. To make him see her point of view, she would have had to explain about her father, and she wasn't ready to do that yet.

"Ready to go down?" Marcie asked from the doorway.

Amanda turned from the window and nodded, realizing that Marcie had been standing there for a moment studying her.

"The mountain starting to get to you too?" asked Marcie.

"Maybe a little," she admitted. "But remember Hazel Wilmot's death didn't have anything to do with that mountain. She died in the Shadsborough Inn."

"Yeah," Marcie muttered. "And what do you want to bet that the inn is somewhere right near the mountain?"

Chapter Four

"Would you like tea, coffee, or cider?" Pat asked as soon as they entered the kitchen. Three large mugs were already set out on the counter.

Amanda opted for raspberry tea, whereas Marcie chose the cider.

The kitchen, which stretched along the entire length of the back of the house, was huge. It felt even more spacious because it had a cathedral ceiling with a skylight centered over a granite countertop big enough for a casual eating area. Stainless steel appliances and industrial lighting gave the room a sleek, modern look that was oddly out of keeping with the rest of the house.

"You said this section was added on in 1925?" Amanda asked, settling in at the counter.

Pat poured the hot water into Amanda's teacup and smiled. "I should have added that we extensively renovated in here when we bought the place. Our theory was that if you're going to be making breakfast for a lot of strangers, you want a kitchen that works well. We serve breakfast for guests in the period dining room, but this is our work space, so function is what counts. Stan and I also updated the furnace and all the wiring. We wanted a place that looked old but worked like new."

Amanda nodded. "When did you take over here?"

"Three years ago." Pat smiled a bit sheepishly. "We had one of those romantic dreams like so many people do that once we retired as teachers we'd buy an old house and run it as a B&B."

"How's it worked out so far?"

Pat shrugged. "We're glad we've both got our pensions to fall back on. Shadsborough attracts its share of tourists in the fall, but it's downright dead the rest of the year. Most of the skiers head to fancier places further up in the mountains, and many of the summer folks want to be nearer to a lake. But at our time in life we don't really want to work that hard anyway."

"Seems like a quiet place," said Amanda.

"It is. Occasionally there's been talk of more development. We really aren't that far from Concord, you know. But so far nothing's come of it. Old families who have been here for generations own most of the land, and none of them are real anxious to sell."

"This cider is great," Marcie interjected.

"Isn't it? It comes from a local orchard. There are some benefits to living in the country."

"You must have moved here about the same time as Professor Wilmot," said Amanda.

Pat nodded. "We even had the same realtor, Randy Markham. Arriving in the village at the same time is why I think we became friends, plus the fact that she lived next door. It also helped that neither one of us was a local, so we could share a good laugh at their expense once in a while."

"Which direction is her house?" asked Marcie.

"The next one that way." Pat pointed down the road away from the mountain.

Amanda spotted a look of relief swiftly passing over Marcie's face.

"You told me on the phone that you were the person who found the note in the kitchen saying that the professor was going to the inn on Saturday night."

"That's right. People don't lock their doors around here, so we would drop in on each other every few days at around ten o'clock in the morning if we needed something or just to chat. I'd knock on the back door or ring the bell. If there was no answer, I'd come into the kitchen and call for Hazel, just to see if everything was all right. Although she seemed to be healthy as a horse, I liked to kind of keep an eye on her since she lived alone."

"I can't imagine her wanting to be looked after very much," said Amanda.

Pat smiled. "She could be crusty and independent. But as long as I didn't fuss, she took it pretty well."

"Did you talk to her on Friday or Saturday?" asked Amanda.

Pat shook her head sadly and held her mug of cider in both hands as if to steady it.

"No. Like I told you yesterday, we had almost a full house over the weekend. I spent Friday getting ready, and then Saturday there were guests under foot all day because it rained. I was at my wit's end trying to keep them entertained. In fact it wasn't until Sunday around noon that I got a chance to bring Hazel her newspaper. We get the Boston papers delivered, and we always get an extra one for Hazel. But she usually stops by herself to pick it up before breakfast."

"So when you didn't see her that morning, you went over to her house?"

Pat stared across the kitchen as if remembering the scene. "I knocked and rang the bell. By then I was starting to realize how long it had been since I had seen her. I got a little worried when there was no answer, especially since her car was parked in the driveway. So I went inside. The kitchen table was cleared except for the note held in place by the salt shaker."

"What did you do next?" Marcie asked, leaning across the counter as the tale became more engrossing.

"I called her name, then I searched the house in case she had come home and not removed the note. When I didn't find her anywhere, I called the police."

Amanda tapped her teaspoon lightly on the hard countertop.

"Do you recall exactly what the note said?"

Pat nodded. "It was short. She'd written 'Saturday Night' in the upper right-hand corner. Then she said, 'Went to the Shadsborough Inn to check things out. Expect to be back soon.' She signed it with her first name."

"Why would she leave a note?" Marcie asked.

Amanda turned to look at her, and Marcie blushed.

"I mean if she expected to be back sometime that night, why leave a note?" she hurried to explain. "She must have expected to be back before you could visit her on Sunday."

"That's a good point," Amanda admitted.

"I'm afraid that the answer is simple," Pat replied. "I do a lot of baking on Saturday night when there are guests staying for the weekend, so lots of times I bring something for Hazel. She might have expected me to come over that night and not have wanted me to worry about her whereabouts. But as it was, I didn't come over until Sunday."

Pat's lips trembled slightly and a tear formed in the corner of one eye. *I guess I don't have a monopoly on guilt*, Amanda thought.

"So when you found she wasn't there, you called the police?"

Pat nodded and composed herself quickly. "Chief Hudson and one of his men went over to the inn and found Hazel."

"And they assumed because the note was still here that she had been there since Saturday night?" asked Marcie.

"And I guess the condition of her body indicated that as well."

"How did she get to the inn if her car was by her house?" asked Amanda.

"It's really not a long walk. You just go back up the hill to the main road through town, then walk north about an eighth of a mile. It's on your left. Hazel was a great one for walking almost everywhere around town."

"Do you have any idea why Professor Wilmot would be looking around in the inn at night?" asked Amanda. "She mentioned something in her message to me about a sobbing sound coming from inside. She also said that some people thought that the inn was haunted."

Shadows had crept across the kitchen while they talked, stretching closer to them as if trying to eavesdrop on the conversation. Pat switched on a set of lights that filled the room with a warm glow.

"I don't really know anything about the so-called legend of the Shadsborough Inn," she said dismissively. "In fact I'd never heard anything about the place being haunted until a week ago. Some boys were walking back to town after dark. One of them saw a light in an upstairs window."

Pat smiled and shrugged. "Being boys they decided to find out what was going on, so they went inside. They claimed they heard a girl crying in the basement. One of them went down the stairs to the cellar and said that there was this mysterious light. He said he saw a girl wearing a nightgown, and she held her hands out to him and said, "Help me! Help me!' Then suddenly the light went out."

Amanda glanced over at Marcie and saw that her eyes were round with a mixture of fear and fascination.

"Probably the boy ran up the stairs as fast as he could as soon as he heard a mouse. Then he made up the rest of it," said Amanda coolly, hoping to diffuse the tension.

Pat frowned. "Could be. But the boy who went downstairs was Jimmy Racine, whose father works for the newspaper down in Concord. He wrote an article for the paper about the incident. I don't think he would have done that if he wasn't pretty certain that Jimmy was telling the truth."

"The whole thing could still have been a hoax," said Amanda.

"That's a pretty elaborate practical joke," Marcie said, then bit her lip when Amanda stared hard at her.

"Country life can get pretty boring, and sometimes young people like to break the monotony with strange pranks," Pat said. "I'd have figured that was all it was myself, if things hadn't gotten a bit more complicated."

"More happened that night?" asked Amanda.

Pat walked across the room and drew the drapes across the windows as if she wanted to keep what she had to say confidential.

"The morning after Jimmy Racine saw this girl or this figment of a girl in the basement, Anne Martin was discovered to be missing."

"Who's she?" asked Marcie.

"A junior in high school. Her folks live about three-quarters of a mile past the inn. She told her parents she was going to visit a friend who lives next door, but she never showed up. The friend was home but didn't see her and knew nothing about her intending to come over."

"Could she have been the girl in the basement of the inn asking for help?" Marcie whispered as if afraid of being overheard.

"It's certainly possible. The inn was only a quarter of a mile away from where her father dropped her off," said Pat.

"But why would she be wandering around this deserted inn in her nightgown?" Amanda asked.

"Maybe it wasn't really her," said Marcie.

Amanda gave her a quizzical glance.

"Well . . . I mean . . . maybe she was already dead, and what this boy saw was an apparition of her asking for help."

Amanda bit back a sharp comment.

Pat smiled ruefully. "There's a story like that already going around the village. I'm not sure who started it, probably Middie Ross."

"Who's she?" asked Amanda.

"Some people call her an herbalist; others say she's a witch." Pat grinned at the startled expression on Marcie's face. "Oh, she's really not scary. She runs an herbal shop in the center of town. We don't have those health-food chains out here, so she sort of fills the gap. But she also carries books and charms that have to do with healing, benevolent witchcraft, and using the 'powers of nature.'

She and Hazel used to get into some fierce arguments on occasion over the virtues of natural healing versus modern medicine."

"If we assume that Anne Martin really was the girl in the basement of the inn and not an apparition," Amanda said, giving Marcie a repressive look, "Then there are two questions: what was she doing there and what happened to her?"

"The state police took over the organization of a full-scale search three days ago. My husband, Stan, is out with them now. They're trying to thoroughly cover the mile or so from Anne's house to town."

"Sounds like a tall order," said Amanda.

"Especially since there are deep woods all along there on both sides of the road, and a lot of trees and bushes still have their leaves. They'll have to look under everything."

"For a body?"

Pat nodded. "If she were still alive, they figure she would have turned up somewhere by now."

"Maybe she ran away from home," Marcie said with a trace of anger in her voice as if she didn't want people to give up too soon on the girl still being alive. "Teenage girls do that all the time if they don't get along with their folks or can't hack school."

"From all accounts," Pat replied, "she was a happy, popular girl. She even had the lead in the play they're doing at the high school for Christmas. She doesn't sound like someone who would run away."

"You never know," Marcie persisted, as if she were talking from personal experience.

"Did Professor Wilmot say anything to you about all this?" Amanda asked.

"I ran into Hazel late Thursday outside of the grocery.

We talked about it briefly. She didn't say much when I asked her what she thought was going on, but she did get this mysterious look, like she knew something that I didn't, and said that the inn was at the heart of everything."

"What did she mean by that?" Marcie asked.

Pat smiled sadly. "Although I considered Hazel a friend, she wasn't one to tell you what she was thinking until she got good and ready. When I asked her what she meant, she just shook her head and said that she had to get more evidence first."

"Evidence of what, I wonder," Amanda said, half to herself. "Did Professor Wilmot have any other friends in town that she might have spoken to about these events?"

"I don't know if they were friends, but since she liked to read, I'm sure she knew Susan Marston, the town librarian, pretty well."

"You have no idea why six days after Jimmy Racine saw the girl in the basement of the inn, Hazel decided to go back there to check around?" Amanda asked.

"I'm afraid not."

Amanda bit her lip, not sure how much she wanted to raise suspicions in Pat Bennett's mind. Then she decided that the direct approach might be the only way to get information.

"Do you think Hazel's death night not have been an accident?"

"What else could it be?" the woman asked, puzzled.

Her eyes widened as she understood the point of the question. "You mean do I think Hazel was murdered?" she asked with a disbelieving smile. "Why would anyone do that?"

"Perhaps it has something to do with the ghost," Amanda suggested.

Pat Bennett shook her head. "Whatever Jimmy saw in that house on Tuesday night had to be some kind of teenage prank. Certainly nothing serious enough to kill someone over."

"And Anne Martin's disappearance?" Amanda asked.

"That's certainly more serious, if she really has been abducted. But surely there's no connection to what happened to Hazel. The kind of man who would attack a young girl is hardly likely to be interested in killing an elderly woman," Pat said with a slight blush.

"Who'll get Professor Wilmot's house now that she's dead?" asked Marcie.

Amanda frowned at the sudden change of topic.

"Well, on the police shows they say that you should always find out who will benefit from a person's death," Marcie answered defensively.

"As far as I know she didn't have any family other than her son, Arthur," Pat replied. "Hazel told me once that he'd inherit everything. And that was quite a lot."

"Was she wealthy?" asked Amanda in surprise. She'd never thought of Professor Wilmot as a wealthy woman or even being interested in that sort of thing.

"From what Hazel said, she earned a good salary most of her life, lived frugally, and invested well. I think there should be quite a nice nest egg."

"Does her son live around here?" asked Amanda.

The woman shook her head. "He lives in the suburbs of Chicago."

"Did he come out to visit his mother?" Marcie asked.

"Yes. He came out several times a year, and I think she would occasionally go out there to see him. But not nearly as often as he came out here."

"So they got along okay?" asked Marcie.

Pat paused to consider her answer. "I think he very much wanted her affection, but Hazel wasn't really a warm woman. She could respect someone with a good mind, although, from what she said on occasion, I think she felt Arthur fell a bit short in that regard. However, I'm not sure that she was really capable of loving anyone. Even though I enjoyed her company, she was always a bit distant. It was almost as if her ability to reason was so large that there wasn't much room left for feeling."

"But Arthur kept trying," Marcie said sadly.

"Yes. I don't think he could help himself."

The back door opened and a tall heavyset man walked into the kitchen. He clapped his hands together to warm them, then took off his jacket and hung it on a coat tree next to the door.

"It doesn't seem cold out. But once the sun goes under you can really get a chill," he said, smiling at the women.

"This is my husband, Stan," Pat said.

When the introductions were finished, Pat asked if the searchers had found any sign of Anne. Stan shook his head.

"We've been over every inch of that stretch. I don't think there's anything out there to find."

"Couldn't she have gotten in a car and been taken somewhere?" asked Amanda.

Stan nodded. "But nobody heard anything unusual that night. Of course, it's a pretty empty area from Anne's house to the middle of the town. Other than the inn, there are only four or five houses, and a couple of them are set way back from the road. I think the captain of the state police is going to call off the search. They'll just hope that if she's still alive, someone will spot her from the picture they've got circulating."

"And if she's dead?" Marcie said.

"Once the leaves are off the trees and bushes, we might find her. You'd be surprised how many people tramp around out in the woods all times of the year," Stan replied.

Everyone stared silently in front of them as if they could imagine what it would be like to unexpectedly come upon a partially decomposed body.

"You're welcome to stay to supper," Pat announced suddenly as if trying to break up the somber mood. "It's leftovers from the weekend, but they're pretty tasty if I do say so myself."

"Thank you, anyway," Amanda said quickly before Marcie, who had an eager expression on her face, could accept the offer. "But we'd like to see a little more of the area. Is there a restaurant in town where we could eat?"

"Not right in town, but Connie's Place is pretty good. You go through the center then head out about three miles north. It looks like a gray clapboard house, but there's a neon sign in front," Stan said with enthusiasm, as if he'd like to skip the leftovers and tag along.

Amanda and Marcie got up and started to leave.

"Breakfast is served in the morning from seven to nine," Pat said. "The downstairs door will be open until eleven. If you're out after that you'll have to ring the bell. One of us will come down and let you in."

"I thought people didn't lock their doors around here," Marcie said.

Pat looked over at a grim-faced Stan and sighed. "We do now."

Chapter Five

"When are we going out to eat?" Marcie asked once they were alone upstairs.

"In fifteen minutes. I just want to give Greg a call, so he knows we're okay." Amanda paused and lowered her voice. "Wear your heaviest coat."

"Why? Are we going somewhere else afterward?"

Amanda put a finger to her lips and nodded toward the downstairs.

"You think they might be spying on us?" Marcie asked incredulously.

"I don't intend to trust anyone in this town more than I have to," Amanda whispered.

Marcie nodded doubtfully, then crossed the hall.

Once in her own room, Amanda punched Greg's number on her cell phone.

"Hi, Greg," she said when he answered.

"Amanda! How are things in the north woods?"

She wondered if he was more worried about this assignment than she had thought. Forced joviality was always a sign with Greg that he was less than relaxed about something.

She managed a laugh. "You know how it is, squirrels and trees. That sort of thing. And wherever there are squirrels, there are nuts."

"Of the human kind?"

"None that I've met so far, but it sounds like there's the usual number of village eccentrics. By the way, something else out of the ordinary happened up here recently. A high school girl went missing the same night that the ghost appeared. They still haven't found her."

There was a pause on the line. "Is her case related to the professor's?"

Amanda filled him in on the story of the sobbing girl.

"So this girl Anne could have been in the inn on the night that she disappeared," Greg said.

"Possibly. Of course, it could have been a different girl or maybe there was no girl at all and the boys just decided to make up a good story."

"What are you going to do next?"

Amanda decided not to mention her plans for the night. There was no point in needlessly worrying Greg. "Tomorrow I'm going to have a chat with Susan Marston, who runs the library. I think I'll send Marcie to see Middie Ross, the town witch."

"Throwing Marcie in at the deep end of the pool, aren't you?"

"I'm hoping that Marcie's natural gullibility will be more appealing to a witch than my skepticism, so maybe she'll talk more freely."

"That makes sense. How's Marcie holding up so far?"

"Fine." Amanda didn't see any reason to tell him that her colleague seemed spooked about being in the woods.

Or that both of them were less than pleased at living under the looming mountain.

"Are you sure everything is going okay?"

"Of course I am," she replied.

"All right," Greg said, sounding doubtful, as if he suspected that something was being kept from him. "Give me another call tomorrow and let me know what you've found out."

"Will do," Amanda said, feeling slightly guilty that she hadn't told him all her plans.

"What are you going to have?" Marcie asked, studying the menu.

It was a single piece of cardboard with lunches on one side and dinners on the back. The entire thing was covered with easy-to-clean laminate. However, the dining room was fancier than the menu. The tables were covered with white table cloths, although there was a sheet of glass on top for easy cleaning. And if the rug on the floor was a little dark with age, at least it gave the room a level of elegance that you wouldn't necessarily expect in a place called Connie's.

"I'm going with the broiled chicken," said Amanda. "It's so simple that I don't think they can do anything bad to it."

"Okay. I'll try the same thing."

After they gave the waitress their order, Marcie leaned across the table with a mischievous gleam in her eye.

"Is it safe to talk here or do you think the candle is bugged?" she said, pointing to the fat red candle glowing in the middle of their table.

Amanda gave her a tolerant smile. "We can talk now."

She knew that Marcie had been bursting to know what

they were going to do tonight as they drove out to the restaurant, but Amanda had fended off her initial question with the comment that "they'd talk at dinner." She'd wanted to study the road, especially the first mile out of town. Amanda had slowed down slightly as they passed a large dark building off to the left.

"Is that the Shadsborough Inn?" Marcie asked in a hollow voice.

"Got to be."

Amanda had been surprised to see how close it was to the street. In her mind's eye she had pictured it at the end of a winding drive, surrounded by overgrown trees with low-hanging branches. But she should have realized that the boys walking home wouldn't have seen lights unless the building was near the road.

As they drove further, she realized that Stan was right. There were few houses along that mile stretch to Anne Martin's house, and most of them were set well back from the road. She wondered at which house the girl's father had dropped her off and what had happened after that.

Marcie insistently leaned even further across the restaurant table so that the candle threw dark shadows over her face, hollowing out her features. "So what do you have planned?"

"We're going to take a look around the Shadsborough Inn tonight," Amanda replied.

"Tonight? Why not wait until the morning?"

"Well, first of all, I don't want people seeing us there. The police probably will take a dim view of folks poking around, and I don't want the village gossips spreading the word around that we're investigating Hazel's death."

"Don't you think Pat has told them already?"

"I asked her not to when we first talked on the phone."

"So you *do* trust her then," Marcie said with a note of triumph.

"Up to a point. But I don't want her to know our every move."

Marcie sat back and looked around the dark dining room as if preparing her soul for the even greater darkness she was going to experience after dinner.

"What's your other reason for going there tonight?" she asked.

"Night is when those boys saw something, and that's when the professor was there." Amanda smiled. "If you're looking for ghosts, there's not much point in going at noon."

"I don't think you're taking this seriously enough," Marcie whispered, but the anger was clear in her voice. "One person is dead, maybe two. And you want us to waltz into this place like there's nothing to worry about. I'm sorry, but I don't find that the least bit funny."

Amanda was instantly contrite. "I'm sorry if I gave you the wrong impression. I am taking this very seriously. Although it's possible that Professor Wilmot did die by accident, the disappearance of this girl makes me more suspicious than ever that there was a crime committed."

"That's not what I meant when I said you weren't taking it seriously."

"What, then?" Amanda asked.

Marcie bit her lip. "You're going to think I'm crazy. But what if there is a supernatural presence involved here?" She paused. "Are we prepared to deal with something like that?"

Amanda sat back in her chair. "Do you really believe in that stuff?" she asked, trying to keep her tone gentle.

"I don't know," Marcie said, waving her hand in exasperation. "I've read all those stories we've published. A lot of them I can see might just be folk tales and others could be fabrications, but some were experienced by so many people that they have to be at least partly true. And what do we really know about this kind of thing? Sure, you're a good reporter and all, but this isn't like covering a normal event. You don't have any background in this."

"Look, Marcie, when we started running this column a year ago, I did my research. I know about the Bridgewater Triangle down in Massachusetts; the voices of the dead near Pomfret, Connecticut, The Fiend of Provincetown; and the stories of Old Slipperyskin among the Penobscots. I've read about The Presence on Mt. Washington, William and Horatio Eddy talking to the dead in 1874, and even the electrocuted heifers in Dummerston in 1984. And, believe me, there are lots more."

"Well," Marcie said after a moment, "doesn't all that make you wonder?"

"Of course it does. But even if you add up all the supernatural happenings that just might pass the basic test of credibility, you have to admit that there are still a lot more natural experiences than supernatural ones. So until my own experience tells me otherwise, I'm always going to assume that an event has a natural explanation rather than one that involves ghosts, poltergeists, or Bigfoot."

Amanda sat back in her seat and took a deep breath. She felt bad at letting herself get irritated by the young woman's willingness to believe.

Marcie gave her a shy smile. "Okay, I take it back; you have thought a lot about this. And I guess I agree with you that just because something is hard to explain doesn't mean I should jump to the conclusion that it's genuinely supernatural."

Amanda returned her smile. "Didn't Sherlock Holmes say something like, 'You begin by eliminating all the possible answers until the one that's left, no matter how absurd, must be the right one.'"

"So you're saying that it *could* be a ghost," Marcie concluded with a grin.

"Only if all the other explanations have been eliminated, and I doubt that's going to happen."

The waitress came with their order. When she walked away, Marcie looked doubtfully at her chicken.

"Something wrong?" Amanda asked.

Marcie shook her head. "It's just that if I'd known that we were going to go prowling around the Shadsborough Inn, I would have ordered beef to keep up my strength."

Two hours later, Amanda and Marcie were hiding behind a bush and looking down a dark driveway at the Shadsborough Inn.

"Are you sure the police are keeping an eye on this place?" Marcie asked.

"It's only a quarter of a mile from the police station, and I expect that even Chief Hudson must be smart enough to know that kids, and maybe some adults, might be tempted to have a look around," Amanda replied.

"Good. I'd hate to think that our little stroll in the dark was for nothing."

When they left the restaurant, Amanda had said that they couldn't very well park by the inn because their car would arouse suspicion, so instead they had driven back almost to the center of town and parked their car down a quiet side street away from any houses. Then they had walked back almost a quarter of a mile. Although it was early October, Amanda was glad she had warned Marcie to wear her heaviest jacket because there was a chilly breeze coming down from the north. For once Marcie's normal office attire of a heavy sweater and sturdy trousers made sense. Amanda had even pulled up the hood on her fleece jacket to keep her ears warm and was glad to be wearing her heavy corduroy slacks.

"How are we going to get inside? Just go up to the front door and turn the handle?" Marcie asked.

"Why not? We may as well check the front door in case the police left it open."

"No sense our both going up there," Marcie said quickly. "I'll check."

Before Amanda could offer to go instead, Marcie slipped down the driveway, staying in the shadows until she reached the porch. There was a quick flash from Marcie's light. A few seconds later, she was back at Amanda's side.

"There are boards nailed up at the top and bottom of the door."

"We'll go around to the back, then," Amanda suggested, stepping out from behind the bush she had used to conceal herself from the road. "Let's move fast until we get behind the building and out of sight."

They headed down a branch of the old gravel driveway that must have once been used to go around to the rear of the inn. A quarter-moon gave them enough light to walk without the flashlight, but Amanda was well aware that the same light also would make them visible to any observant driver who happened to pass by. Fortunately, they were well behind the inn before a car passed.

"Should I see if this is open?" Marcie asked, approaching a door at the back.

"Give it a try," Amanda suggested.

Marcie turned the handle and gave a hard pull. Then she pushed. Nothing happened.

"Either it's locked or stuck."

"Let's see if we can get in through a window. I doubt that they all have locks on them, and even if they do, the police probably didn't bother to check every one."

The three windows in the back of the house wouldn't budge no matter how hard the women tried. Between the windows, there was small door cut into the foundation of the house about a foot above the ground.

"What do you think that is, an entrance for elves?" Marcie asked.

"The inn was probably heated with a coal furnace at one time. That's probably where the chute down to the coal bin was," Amanda replied. "A house my folks once rented in Boston had one."

Marcie reached down and pushed on the door.

"It won't give. Maybe I could kick it in. But I suppose it doesn't matter, I'd never fit through it anyway. Although you could give it a shot."

"I think I'll pass."

A set of wooden doors covered a hatchway down into the cellar, but that too refused to open. They walked around the side of house away from the driveway. A wooden storage building that probably had once been used for firewood jutted out from the side of the house. Its flat top went up at a forty-five-degree angle, ending right under a second-floor window. The structure was about five feet high at the lowest end.

"That's too high for me to get on top of or I'd check out that window," said Amanda.

"Let me give you a boost," Marcie offered. She bent down and formed her hands into a sling. "Just put your foot in there and I'll lift you."

"Are you sure? I'm afraid I'll hurt your hands."

"They've been through a lot worse in field hockey," Marcie said.

Amanda put her foot in Marcie's hands and felt herself quickly propelled upward. She easily scrambled on top of the bin. Fortunately the lid seemed to be solid.

"Are you okay?" she whispered down to Marcie.

"Fine. But I'll be a whole lot better if you can get that window open so we can look around and then get the heck out of here."

Amanda walked up along the angled top of the bin toward the window. She slipped once on the shingled surface and was glad that she had on the corduroys to help protect her knees. When she reached the window, she squatted down and put her hands firmly on the sash and lifted. It squeaked and moved up about an inch. She braced herself even more, got her hands in the open space, and pulled up. After three more attempts it had grudgingly opened about two feet. Still not much, but enough for Amanda to slide inside.

"I'm going in," she called down to Marcie.

"Not without me," Marcie replied. "Reach down and give me a lift up."

"You don't have to," Amanda said, although she had to admit to herself that entering the big empty building alone made her a little nervous.

"Don't argue," Marcie said with new authority in her voice.

Amanda returned to the lower end of the bin and

extended her hand, expecting that it would be difficult to pull the heavier woman up onto the bin, but Marcie quickly scrambled up with little help.

"You are athletic," Amanda said.

"Told you."

They approached the window again. Amanda turned on the flashlight and peered around inside the room before entering.

"What do you see?" asked Marcie.

"Nothing. The room looks to be empty. I'll go in first," said Amanda.

She lifted her right leg over the sill and disappeared inside. Marcie heard a dull thump.

"Are you okay?"

"Yeah, the window is a little way above the floor, so be careful of the drop."

Amanda held the flashlight beam toward the floor, so Marcie could see as she came inside. She dropped to the floor with enviable grace.

They used their flashlights to scan the room. It was empty except for a three-legged wooden chair that leaned drunkenly against one wall. Amanda walked to a door and slowly opened it. It led out into a hall that extended off in both directions. She sent the beam of the flashlight to her right and then to her left. The peeling wallpaper that hung from the walls like shedding skin and the decaying carpet made it look like the caricature of a haunted house. Amanda shivered slightly and could understand why the boys might have well imagined that they heard someone sobbing.

"Where do we go next?" asked Marcie.

"Well, I guess since we're in here we should take a look around the entire place."

"I suppose," Marcie answered doubtfully.

"To do it quickly, I guess it would be best if we split up."

"I was afraid you were going to suggest that."

"How about you look in the rooms on this floor. I'll check out the downstairs and the basement."

"Sure. But what if I meet you downstairs, and we do the basement together?"

"Are you sure?" Amanda asked.

"Yeah. Probably there's no ghost. And if there is, well, I guess we'd better face it together."

Amanda gave Marcie's hand a squeeze. "I'll wait for you at the bottom of the stairs after I check out the first floor." She used the beam of the flashlight to point to her left. "The stairs must be that way, toward the front of the house."

Marcie nodded and went down the hall in the opposite direction toward the back of the house. Amanda headed left and eventually came to wide staircase. She slowly went down the stairs, examining each step carefully to make sure that it was secure. Falling through the staircase to the floor below would certainly get their investigation off on the wrong foot, Amanda thought with a grim smile.

When she reached the downstairs hallway and what appeared to be the front door, there were rooms off the hall in both directions. She began with the one to the right of the front door. The door creaked open to reveal a large, empty room with a brick fireplace filling one wall. Although all of the furniture was gone, she surmised that it had probably been the main parlor. Amanda crossed the space and opened the door to another room in the back that was only slightly smaller, with two windows at one end. Amanda guessed that it had been a dining room because as she went through a swinging door in the far corner, she found herself in the kitchen.

Amanda stopped for a moment, surprised to have come upon a room that actually had something in it. She studied the appliances that had been new a half-century ago, and wondered why the owners hadn't sold them when they shut down the inn. Standing in the center of the room, Amanda let the beam of her flashlight travel around the walls looking for doors. One door clearly led back out to the main hall and another was definitely a back door that went to the outside. A narrower door probably indicated a closet or pantry. Finally the light settled on a door in the far corner of the room. Pat had told her that the boys had gotten into the cellar from the kitchen, so this must be the way down, Amanda concluded.

The thought of not waiting for Marcie and having a quick look around in the basement tempted her for a moment. After all, she was already almost there and most likely she had nothing to fear. But Amanda didn't want to hurt Marcie's feelings. She knew that going down in the cellar was the last thing that Marcie wanted to do and that by agreeing to accompany her, Marcie was demonstrating her commitment to the job and to Amanda herself. It wouldn't be right not to treat that with respect.

Reluctantly, Amanda went through the door that led back out to the main hall. As she was walking up the hall, Amanda heard a rubbing sound coming from the vicinity of the front door, as if an animal of some kind were trying to get inside. Suddenly there was a loud thump. Not sure what was happening, Amanda decided to head back upstairs to warn Marcie, but just as she reached the first step, the front door opened wide, and she was caught in a beam of light.

Not sure whether to go upstairs or back down the hall

to the kitchen, she paused for an instant. A grunt of surprise came from the doorway and a nasal male voice shouted, "Hey you!" As she turned to run upstairs, he shoved her from behind and Amanda fell forward onto the steps. An arm grabbed her around the waist and began to pull her down to the hallway.

"Help!" she managed to call out, hoping that Marcie would hear. Then she twisted around and poked an elbow into whoever was behind her. She had an instant of satisfaction in feeling it connect and hearing her attacker let out a yelp of pain.

The grip round her waist loosened momentarily. She tried to break free, but he grabbed her again and pulled her down to the floor. She twisted onto her back and rammed the heel of her hand forward to where she guessed his face would be. It was only a glancing blow, and he caught her hand the next time she tried it.

"Stop that," he said in a complaining voice as if she were attacking him.

He pinned both her hands by her sides and she could feel his warm breath on her cheek. Bracing herself, she moved forward quickly with her forehead and felt it strike his face. He squealed.

"Don't do that!"

Amanda was exhausted and lay still, trying to think of what to do next. He wasn't that strong or tough. If only she could get some leverage, she might be able to escape, but his weight was pressing down on her chest, making it hard for her to breathe.

"Get off me," she said.

"Not until you tell me what I want to know. Now I'm going to ask you some questions and I expect—"

Before he finished his sentence there was a flash of light over Amanda's head and suddenly the pressure on her chest was gone.

"Are you all right?" Marcie asked, bending over her.

"Yeah. I guess. What happened?"

"I hit him on the head with my flashlight. I think it's broken. Do you know where yours is?"

"I dropped it at the bottom of the steps when he tackled me."

"I'll go get it."

"Be careful. He's still around here somewhere," Amanda said, scrambling to her feet and holding onto the railing for support.

"Yeah, he's right here on the floor next to you, but it doesn't sound like he's moving," Marcie said, bending over. "I hope that I didn't kill him."

A few seconds later a flashlight went on by the front door and rapidly approached Amanda.

"Found it," Marcie announced.

"Let's see what we've got here," said Amanda.

Marcie shined the light on the floor, and Amanda made out the form of a thin man not much taller than herself, lying on his side. Amanda almost smiled to herself at how he seemed to be peacefully sleeping, but her face hardened when she thought about how he had attacked her.

"Is he alive?" Marcie asked nervously.

"I'm not sure how we can tell. Let's try to wake him up. I think the two of us can easily handle him while he's still groggy."

She reached down, and with Marcie's help, rolled him onto his back. She shoved the flashlight close to his face. He looked to be in his early thirties with sharp features and a receding chin. She was wondering what color his eyes were when, as if on cue, they opened and suddenly she could see they were brown.

"What happened?" he mumbled, propping himself up on one elbow and reaching his other hand behind his head. He touched a spot gingerly and groaned. "Someone hit me."

"My friend hit you because you were attacking me. And you'd better lie still because if you start any more trouble you'll just get hurt worse," Amanda said, backing away as he climbed slowly to his feet.

"Who are you?" he demanded sullenly.

"Who are you?" Amanda asked, feeling slightly childish at repeating his question.

"I'm Arthur Wilmot."

"The son of Professor Wilmot?" Amanda asked.

"Did you know my mother?" he asked, moderating the harshness of his tone slightly.

"I was a student of hers."

"What are you doing here?"

"That's kind of a long story—"

"And I think you should save it for another time," Marcie broke in from where she was standing by the still open front door. She switched off her flashlight. "I think I just saw a police cruiser pull up."

"Is your car out there?" Amanda asked the man.

"No. It's down the road hidden under some trees."

"Okay. Let's get out of here, then," said Amanda. "Marcie, switch on the flashlight but keep your hand over the upper part of it, so it doesn't show as much. You lead the way back to where we came in."

Letting only a narrow beam of light shine on the stairs, Marcie quickly led the way up the steps.

"This is the police. Is someone in here?" They heard a

voice call from the front door as they slipped into the upstairs room.

Marcie led the way out the window, and Amanda whispered directions to Arthur Wilmot. The three of them scrambled out onto the top of the woodbin and edged their way down the sloped surface to the end. Amanda glanced quickly toward the front of the house, expecting to see the police coming around the corner with flashlights and drawn guns. She heard Marcie jump from the top of the bin and land softly on the ground.

"It's only about five feet. Keep your knees loose and you'll be okay," Marcie whispered back to Arthur.

"You go next," Arthur Wilmot said, roughly pushing Amanda forward in front of him. "I'm afraid of heights."

"Okay," Amanda said. "But if you don't jump right after me, you'll be explaining things to the police."

"Don't worry, I'll jump."

Marcie put the flashlight on for an instant, so Amanda could see where to land. Suddenly the five feet seemed like the top of a skyscraper. Knowing that hesitation would only make things worse, she jumped forward off the top of the bin, trying to remember to keep her knees slightly bent to absorb the shock. The impact of hitting the ground sent a jolt of pain up her legs and into her back, but she didn't think anything had been damaged.

"You okay?" Marcie whispered in her ear.

"Yes. Give Arthur a look at the ground."

Marcie put on the flashlight for a second.

"Let's go, Arthur," Amanda urged.

There was no reply.

"You have to jump now!"

There was silence.

"Is he still up there?" Amanda whispered to Marcie.

Marcie turned on the flashlight again and directed the beam up to the top of the bin. Arthur Wilmot was poised on the edge, staring straight ahead, frozen in place. When Marcie turned her light off, Amanda could see another light coming into the room they had just left. She knew that in a few seconds the police officer would figure out where they had gone.

"Jump or we'll leave you, Arthur," Amanda threatened.

When there was still no response, Amanda said, "Let's grab him behind his legs and pull him off."

"He could get hurt," Marcie warned.

But Amanda had already grabbed him by the left calf, and between the two of them they gave him a hard pull. With a yelp he leaped forward, hitting the ground hard. He immediately groaned.

"My ankle. I think it's sprained."

"Can you stand up?" Amanda asked.

As he struggled to his feet, Amanda and Marcie stood on either side to support him.

"Let's get into those trees," Amanda said, looking in the direction of clump of woods about fifty feet behind the inn.

A beam of light came out the upstairs window.

"What's going on down there?" a voice shouted.

"Let's move," Amanda said, staying close to the house where they'd be harder to spot. With each woman holding up a side, they managed to half-walk, half-drag Arthur Wilmot across the open area and into the trees.

"Can we rest now?" he asked in a hoarse voice, as soon as they were out of sight of the inn.

"Let's go a little farther," Marcie said, "in case that cop tries to follow us."

They stopped when Amanda finally had to admit that

she was out of breath and couldn't carry the man another step. They paused to listen in case they were being followed.

"Do you think he got a look at us?" Marcie asked, stared behind them into the darkness of the woods as if expecting to momentarily see the flashlight beam of a pursuer.

"I don't think so," Amanda said. "We stayed in the darkness by the side of the house."

"Then maybe he'll think it was just a bunch of kids and not bother to follow us," Marcie said, relaxing a bit.

Amanda bent over Arthur Wilmot, who had slumped down on the ground as soon as they released him. "How's the ankle?"

"I don't know."

Amanda borrowed Marcie's flashlight. Partially covering the beam, she pulled his sock down to the bottom of his shoe and examined the foot.

"Can you move your foot?"

He obediently rotated it.

"It only hurts when I walk on it," he said.

"Good thing it's his left foot. At least he can drive," said Marcie.

"It might be a little swollen," Amanda said after a quick examination. "Rest when you get home and put some ice on it if it swells more."

"Swells more?" he asked in a weak tone.

Marcie patted him hard on the back. "Don't worry, Artie, you'll be fine."

"My name is Arthur."

"Whatever."

"Now how about telling us what you were doing in the

inn?" Amanda asked. "And don't ask me what I was doing there."

"My mother's dead. I wanted to find out what happened. That incompetent chief of police keeps saying that it was just an accident, but I don't believe that for a minute. You knew my mother; do you think she'd fall down a flight of stairs?"

"Did you find anything at the inn?" Amanda asked, wanting to stay in the role of questioner.

"How could I? You saw me come in. I didn't get a chance to look around."

Amanda paused for a moment. "But this wasn't the first time you've been in there, was it? I mean, the police must have called you on Sunday afternoon to tell you that your mother had died. So you probably caught a flight out of Chicago to Boston on Monday morning. I'll bet with a little luck you were out here by yesterday afternoon."

"So? That doesn't mean I went looking around the inn."

"The front door looked to be boarded up. But when you came in the inn tonight you didn't have a hammer or crowbar in your hands. I'll bet that's because you came out Monday night and took the boards off. Then you put them back loosely, so the door would still look boarded up. Did you find something when you were here last night? A clue to what happened to your mother?"

"I want to go home now," he said sullenly.

Amanda decided that the truth might motivate him to cooperate. "Look, your mother called me and left a message about the ghost in the basement of the inn. I work for *Roaming New England* magazine, and she thought there might be a good story about the place."

"A ghost story. My mother didn't believe in stuff like that," the man protested.

"I suspect she planned to get to the bottom of it and reveal what was really going on. That's why she was in the basement that night."

"Okay, that's enough," Arthur Wilmot said irritably. "I don't want to talk any more tonight. I'm cold, my ankle hurts, my head is sore, and I want some time to think about things. I'm staying at my mother's house. Come by tomorrow at eleven and maybe I'll talk to you."

Figuring that was the most she was going to get, Amanda helped Arthur to his feet, then she and Marcie supported him as they walked through the woods to the road. Fortunately they came out not far from the spot where he had hidden his car. Once they had gotten him behind the wheel, Amanda leaned down by the open window.

"See you tomorrow," she said.

Without responding, Wilmot stepped on the gas and pulled away quickly.

"What a jerk," Marcie said. "He almost gets us caught by the police, we carry him halfway across the country-side, and then gravel in the face is all the thanks we get."

The two women began walking back to the center of the village. They ducked into the woods whenever they heard a car approach, just in case the police were still on the lookout for the intruders.

"That was pretty good the way you figured out that Art had been in the inn before," Marcie said after a long silence.

"It was a lucky guess. It could just have been that the police did a poor job of boarding up."

"Do you really think that he found anything last night when he looked around?"

"I'm betting he did or else he wouldn't have come back tonight. He probably has a clue of some sort, but doesn't know what to do with it."

"Will we?"

Amanda smiled. "Well, you know what they say about three heads being better than one."

"What do you make of Arthur?" Marcie asked a few minutes later. "Aside from his being a jerk."

"From what Pat told us, he's a guy who never lived up to what his mother expected, so I figure that right now he feels that he's got one more chance to prove himself by finding out what happened to her."

"He's not exactly an action hero."

"No. But I expect he's doing the best he can."

They reached their car without further incident and drove back to where they were staying. Amanda checked her watch as they pulled in the driveway and was relieved to see that they had a half-hour before the front door would be locked. She didn't want them getting off on the wrong foot with Pat Bennett. They opened the front door quietly and slipped inside so they wouldn't disturb their hostess. They were both scratched and disheveled and didn't want to answer any questions.

"I'm beat," Marcie said as they climbed the stairs to their rooms. "What time are we going down to breakfast?"

"How about eight-thirty?"

"Okay. Bang hard on my door if I don't answer."

"You can use the bathroom first tonight," Amanda said, opening her door.

"Thanks, Sis," Marcie replied.

Amanda grinned. "And by the way, you did a really good job boosting me up onto the roof tonight. I'd never have made it without you. And you really came on like the Marines when Art had me pinned on the floor. I want to thank you."

"No thanks needed." Marcie paused in the doorway of her room studying the floor. "You know I was really scared about going to the inn. I guess that sounds silly to you."

"Not really. There was no telling what we'd find. Look at Arthur Wilmot; he was pretty scary for a while there."

"Guys don't frighten me. If I can touch it, I can fight it. But this ghost business gives me the creeps."

Amanda shrugged. "Some people are more inclined to believe that stuff than others. Maybe it just shows that you have a more active imagination that I do."

Marcie smiled faintly at Amanda's attempt to smoothe over their differences. "I was wondering whether you've ever read anything about ghosts of women crying in basements."

Amanda frowned. "Not exactly. But I think I remember something about a baby sobbing in the rooms of the Bowman Mansion in Cuttingsville, Vermont, and in the eighteenth century there was a house in Maine where the ghost of a dead girl talked to people in the basement."

"To *people*? You mean more than one."

"Yeah. I think she talked to a whole lot of people, if you believe the story."

"Swell," Marcie said, closing her door. "I'm really glad that I asked."

Chapter Six

At seven-thirty the next morning, Amanda pulled her yellow terry cloth robe around her and walked out of her room and down the hall to the bathroom. She almost stumbled over Marcie in shorts and a sweatshirt doing stretches in the hallway.

"I thought you were going to sleep late," Amanda mumbled, still bleary-eyed.

"I woke up early, so I figured that I might as well go out for a run."

"What time was that?"

"Around six-thirty. The sun was just coming up."

Amanda shook her head in amazement. "It must have been cold."

"Yeah. It was a little nippy," Marcie said with the casualness of someone used to physical challenges.

"Did you happen to run past Hazel Wilmot's house?"

Marcie grinned. "I made a point of it. And Art's car was parked in the driveway, so at least that much of what he told us was true."

"See anything else interesting?"

"I took a turn through the town center. I spotted the library and the herbal shop. Can you believe that it's called Herbal Help? But I didn't see a soul around except for a milkman. They must still make deliveries around here. And I didn't run out past the inn. Not because I was afraid to go there, at least not in daylight, but because I didn't want to run the risk of getting spotted by any cops hanging around the place."

"Good idea," Amanda replied, not sure that she quite accepted Marcie's reason for avoiding the inn. "So I'll see you at eight-thirty, then."

"Sure. By the way, are we going to tell Pat Bennett about going out to the Shadsborough Inn last night?"

Amanda shook her head. "We'll keep quiet on that until we have a better sense of what's going on around here."

"And what are we going to do after breakfast?"

"I gave some thought to that last night. I think we should split up to save time. We need to talk to Susan Marston, the librarian. And we should also have a chat with ~~Middle~~ Ross."

"The witch," Marcie said, narrowing her eyes. "Why do I have a premonition that I'm going to be the one to visit her?"

Amanda smiled. "If you're already having premonitions, I think that makes you the ideal person to interview her."

"Do I have to?" Marcie asked. "Couldn't I be the one to talk to the nice, safe librarian?"

Amanda pulled her robe more tightly around her, realizing how hard it was to be in command when you were wearing something that was yellow and fuzzy.

"The way to get information from this woman is by appearing sympathetic to her ideas. Now which one of us do you think is more likely to come across that way?"

Marcie frowned. "You're just saying that I appear naïve."

"No. I'm saying that you look like a young woman right out of college who might be open to alternative therapies for whatever is ailing you."

"What's ailing me?"

Amanda sighed in exasperation. "Make something up. Tell her you work in front of a computer all day and get headaches; say you need a cure for writer's cramp, or hangnails. No matter what you come up with, I'm sure she'll have some kind of flower or weed that she'll claim is a sure cure for it."

"Well," Marcie said, looking prim, "I can see with that kind of a negative attitude you certainly won't get far with the woman."

"Exactly my point. So you'll go talk to her?"

"Sure. No problem."

"Great."

Only when she got into the bathroom and heard a small laugh as the door started to close did she realize that Marcie had been teasing her.

"Young subordinates," Amanda muttered as she turned on the shower.

They went down to the dining room right on the dot of eight-thirty. Amanda poked her head into the kitchen just so Pat Bennett would know they were there. The woman was sitting at the counter with a mug of coffee, reading the paper.

"Good morning," she said in response to Amanda's greeting. "Did you sleep well?"

Amanda assured her that they had slept fine and commented on the ornate decorations in the guestrooms.

"My taste runs to contemporary minimalist," Pat said, smiling. "Our bedroom is mostly glass and metal. But people who come to a B&B in the country expect to see quilts on the bed and antiques cluttering up the room."

"You have to give the customers what they want." Amanda's eyes drifted to the newspaper. "Is there anything new?"

"This is the Boston paper. If you mean locally, Stan was up to the police station this morning already, just to see if they were going to be searching for Anne today; but, as he expected, the state authorities have called it off. And there was a little ruckus out at the Shadsborough Inn last night."

"Oh?" Amanda struggled to keep her expression neutral.

"I guess some kids took the boards off the front door and were looking around inside. Jeremy Cooper, on the night patrol, spotted them and chased them away." Pat paused and smiled. "Of course, since Jeremy is about fifty pounds overweight, I doubt that he chased them very hard."

Amanda smiled politely, saying a silent word of thanks that the officer on the scene hadn't been a champion sprinter.

"According to Stan, the chief was going out there this morning to secure the place better."

Amanda groaned to herself. Now it would be even harder to get inside the inn, and she still wanted to take a look at the place where Hazel Wilmot had died.

"Why don't you and Marcie have a seat out in the dining room? There are menus on the table. Pick anything you want. If you don't see something that you want, just ask. I only stick to the menu when we have a crowd."

Amanda went back to the dining room and sat across from Marcie, who was reading a copy of the *Boston Globe* that was provided for guests.

"Any new information?" Marcie whispered.

Amanda quickly brought her up to date.

"Don't worry," Marcie assured her. "If they only have one guy on patrol at night, we'll still be able to get into the inn. We'll just have to bring something to pry open a door or window."

Amanda nodded, slightly surprised at her colleague's aggressive approach to breaking and entering. Pat came out and asked them what they would like to drink. Amanda asked for coffee, while Marcie opted for a glass of milk.

"You don't drink coffee?" Amanda asked.

"Never developed a taste for it." Marcie picked up on Amanda's surprised expression. "Is it a requirement for investigative journalism?"

"Not at all. I guess it's just that everyone I've worked with has pretty much had a coffee cup attached to their hand most of the day."

Marcie smiled. "I'm high-strung enough. I don't need coffee nerves."

Marcie ordered the blueberry pancakes, while Amanda asked for one egg poached and an order of wheat toast without butter.

"I can see how you stay so thin."

"I'm not thin, I'm slender," Amanda corrected her.

"Yeah. And I always say that I'm solidly built."

The two women shared a smile.

When the coffee came it was piping hot and had a deep, rich taste. The thickly sliced toast had several different grains in it and was sweetened with honey. Marcie declared that the pancakes were the best she'd had since eating in her mother's kitchen back in Nebraska.

When Pat came back to refill her coffee, Amanda asked, "Did you know that Arthur Wilmot is in town?"

"Yes. Stan told me that he saw him at the police station."

"Do you happen to remember what day that was?"

She nodded. "It was Monday afternoon, because I commented to Stan that Arthur was lucky to have gotten a flight out here so quickly."

When Pat returned to the kitchen, Marcie smiled over her glass of milk at Amanda.

"So you figured it right. Arthur was out to the house once already on Monday night."

"We can't be sure of that, but I certainly wouldn't be surprised."

"Could he have had anything to do with his mother's death?" asked Marcie.

"Just because he stood to inherit?"

Marcie nodded.

"I doubt it," Amanda said. "She was his mother, after all, and when the police called him that night, he was in Chicago."

"But that was the day after Hazel was killed. He could have flown out here on Friday, killed her on Saturday, and been home before the body was discovered on Sunday."

Amanda drank the last of her coffee. "I'll admit that the logistics are possible, but do you really see him having the nerve to kill somebody?"

"What did you think last night when he was wrestling with you?"

Amanda paused. "I really didn't think he was trying to kill me. But even if he did murder his mother, why would he come back to the inn last night? Was he looking for something that might incriminate him?"

"Sure. Maybe he got scared off the night he killed her and came back to check around."

"I suppose it's possible, although I don't know why he'd set up an elaborate plan using a supposed ghost at the inn," Amanda said, standing up. "Plus I think he was anxious to get his mother's affection, not her money."

"But he stays on the suspect list?" Marcie said.

"So far he's the only one with a motive."

Amanda stepped into the kitchen to thank Pat Bennett for breakfast. The woman was sitting at the counter, still reading the paper over a cup of coffee.

"Where are the two of you off to?" she asked.

"We thought we'd talk to a few of the people Hazel spent some time with shortly before she died."

Pat Bennett put her paper down and gave Amanda a level look. "You told me about Hazel calling you to talk about the Shadsborough Inn, but I'm not completely clear about what you hope to discover. We'll never know what idea Hazel may have had about the haunting, and even if it was some kind of joke or scam, surely Hazel's death will have put an end to it. No one will be playing any pranks around the inn after that."

"I don't know what we'll find, if anything. But I feel a responsibility to Professor Wilmot to at least find out as much as possible about what led up to her death," Amanda replied.

She had no difficulty making her sense of guilt sound genuine, because it was. Amanda hoped that her display of emotion would keep Pat from probing further into her motives. The more people thought that she was simply gathering information about her friend's tragic accident, the easier everything would go.

But Pat's next question showed that she wasn't so easily misled.

"You asked me last night if I thought Hazel was murdered. Do you think so?"

"I don't have any more information than you do. Based on that, I think you're right that there's no good reason to think that Hazel was murdered."

No good reason other than the fact that I can't conceive of Hazel Wilmot falling down the stairs, Amanda thought.

"But you're going to look into it anyway?" the woman asked with a shrewd glint in her eye.

"I think I owe her that much."

Pat nodded. "I understand. But be careful. What worries me more than the ghost is the fact that Anne Martin is missing. I think that means there's someone out there who's very dangerous."

Chapter Seven

Marcie walked up the street and stopped by the front door of Herbal Help. Unfortunately the lights were on and a large WELCOME sign hung in the front window. Marcie had been half-hoping that the shop would be closed, so she could at least postpone what promised to be an awkward interview. After all, who knew whether witches kept regular business hours or if today might not happen to be some pagan holiday? Seeing that today was apparently a witches' workday, she resigned to her fate and went inside.

Marcie was surprised to find that instead of a darkly lit cottage reminiscent of *Hansel and Gretel*, the shop was bright and cheerful. The rows of shelves to her left and right were filled with bottles that seemed no more mysterious than what you would find in the average pharmacy or health food store, and the woman standing behind the counter wasn't dressed in black and sporting a pointy hat. In fact she was wearing a gray blouse and dark blue skirt, looking very trim and fit. With the string of pearls at her neck and hoop earrings, Marcie thought she looked more prepared to attend a fancy luncheon than dole out eye of newt. All in all, she looked very well put together for a woman that Marcie figured was about the age of her grandmother.

The blue eyes she turned on Marcie were sharp and intelligent, making the young woman feel as if she were being examined.

"May I help you?" the woman asked, giving Marcie a polite smile.

"I'm not sure," Marcie replied.

She had run down a list of possible ailments to tell the woman in order to get a conversation going, ranging from migraine headaches to a sore throat, but as she walked toward the counter, the woman said, "You're limping slightly on your right leg."

"I am?" Marcie said. She stopped to think about it and realized that she had felt some tightness around her knee as she'd been running that morning and that it still had a sore, achy feeling. "Yeah. I guess it hurts a little."

The woman came out from around the counter, her heels clicking efficiently on the tile floor. As she drew closer, Marcie could read a badge similar to the kind nurses in the hospital wore that said MIDDIE ROSS.

"Here's some Saint-John's-wort," Middie said, taking a bottle from the shelf. "This is good for bone cartilage and for tendon and ligament health."

"Yeah," Marice said, pretending to study the bottle. "This sounds like just what I need."

"Now you don't seem absolutely certain as to what's bothering you," the woman said, moving over to another shelf. "That might mean that you're generally feeling a bit run down. I'd recommend echinacea for that. It will help build up your general immune system."

Another bottle was thrust at Marcie, which she dutifully pretended to read.

"Now a young woman like you might also have need for this," Middle continued, thrusting a bottle labeled PAS-SION FLOWER at her. She smiled slightly. "I guess you can figure out the benefits from that."

Marcie blushed and handed the passion flower back to the woman. "Maybe after my leg is feeling better," she said, knowing that sounded stupid, but she wasn't about to discuss her sex life with a woman old enough to be her grandmother. Plus, she was desperate to get out of the shop without spending a week's salary. "I guess that will be all for today."

Middie nodded and led Marcie back to the counter.

As the woman punched the prices into the cash register, Marcie pretended to notice her name for the first time. "I guess you're Middie Ross."

"That's right," the woman said, pausing to give her a long look.

"I'm staying down at Pat Bennett's place. She mentioned your shop to me as a place to see."

"That just goes to show that there aren't many places to see in Shadsborough," the woman said with another small smile.

"I guess that's true."

"Are you touring the area?" Middie asked grudgingly, giving the impression that small talk didn't come to her easily.

"I'm here with someone who was a friend of Hazel Wilmot's."

"Oh, yes. A shame about Hazel."

The words had a flat quality that made Marcie wonder how sincerely they were meant.

"I guess she was a customer here."

Middie Ross concentrated on putting Marcie's items in a bag, and didn't say anything until she handed them across the counter to Marcie.

"She came in here a lot, but I wouldn't call her a customer." A quick frown passed over her face, making her features suddenly seem more pointed. "In fact, you might call her the anti-customer. Hazel only came into the shop when she had an article to show me about some study purportedly debunking the value of herbal treatments."

"That couldn't have been good for business," Marcie blurted out.

"To give Hazel her due, she always waited until only the two of us were in the shop, and she never continued our discussions if a customer entered." Middie paused, then said a bit wistfully, "I have to admit that I rather enjoyed our back and forths over the benefits of holistic medicine, and I think Hazel did as well. It was probably the only opportunity she got in the village to actually have an intelligent argument with someone."

"So you didn't argue about religion?" asked Marcie.

Middie gave her a puzzled look, then laughed. It was a harsh, barking sound that made Marcie take a step back.

"You've probably heard about that witch thing. You only have to stop for a moment in town and someone is pointing me out as the local old crone. Shows how boring rustic life can be. It's true I practice Wicca, but that doesn't mean I'm casting evil spells or making pacts with Satan. Hazel was one of the few folks around who was open-minded enough to realize that. She didn't agree with my beliefs, but at least she was willing to discuss them rationally with me."

"Did she talk to you about what happened to those boys out at the old Shadsborough Inn?"

Middie frowned and shook her head in puzzlement.

"That was one thing that we strongly disagreed about. When I first heard about it, I thought that perhaps the energy of a girl who had died in the inn many years ago suddenly had manifested herself for some reason. You read about that quite a lot in the literature of paranormal events. Hazel heard that I had said that to someone, and she came into the store as angry as I'd ever seen her. She said I was a bigger fool than she thought I was if I believed claptrap like that. I tried to cite all the studies I was aware of on the subject and told her that I wasn't saying this was definitely a ghostly manifestation. But she refused to listen to me and stormed out. That was the Friday before she died, and the last time I saw her."

"Do you know why she was so angry?"

"No. But everyone was starting to get a bit on edge because of Anne Martin disappearing, and Hazel seemed to believe that the two events were connected."

"Why do you say that?"

Middie tugged on one of her earrings. "The last thing she said to me before she walked out was that this thing may have started as an attempt to promote a belief in the supernatural for financial purposes, but if a girl had been harmed, she would guarantee that the people responsible would pay."

"Do you think she blamed you for Anne's disappearance?"

The woman's face stiffened. "If she did, then she was wrong. And you would be, too," she replied in a tone that told Marcie it was time to go.

Shadsborough Library was situated in the short row of buildings in the center of town that included the police station and the village hall; however, no attempt had been made to achieve any kind of architectural consistency. The police station was a functional building made of concrete block and glass, probably constructed in the 1970s. The village hall looked like a miniature castle made sometime in the early part of the twentieth century out of stone and mortar. In between these two the library was nestled, a white clapboard house that had obviously once been someone's home with a broad front porch and a cozy, welcoming look.

Amanda went inside and was pleased to see that there were nicely kept hardwood floors in the entryway that led up to the librarian's desk in the room to the right. In the room to the left were shelves of books. Directly in front of her she saw a sign saying CHILDREN'S ROOM, pointing to the rear of the building. Behind the desk a woman of around her own age had open books piled one on top of the other. She was busily typing entries into a computer. When Amanda walked to the desk, the shiny hardwood floor creaking with every step she took, the woman mumbled something and glared at the computer.

"Not as much help as they're supposed to be?" Amanda asked sympathetically.

The woman smiled. "Once you get the information into them, they're fine. But they're pretty fussy about how you put in the information. Do it a little bit differently than it should be done, and they spit it right back at you."

Amanda watched her type information from the flyleaf into the boxes on the computer screen. She was a couple of inches taller than Amanda's five-seven, with chestnut brown hair that was pulled back into a prim bun. Amanda imagined that she would be very pretty with her hair down and wondered if the woman purposely made herself fit the traditional image of the staid librarian. In a town like Shadsborough, outdated stereotypes might still apply.

"Sorry for the delay," she said, pressing the ENTER key with a mixture of authority and relief. "How can I help you?"

"Are you Susan Marston?"

"That's right."

Amanda introduced herself and mentioned that she was staying at Pat Bennett's.

"I'm an old friend of Hazel Wilmot's."

"Wasn't that a tragedy?" Susan said. "I just couldn't believe it when I heard about it. Hazel was such a fit and capable woman for her age. How could she ever have fallen down the stairs, even in that dumpy old inn?"

"I wondered the same thing myself," said Amanda.

The librarian gave her an appraising glance. "You said you were a friend of Hazel's. Are you in town to find out what happened to her?"

"What do you mean?" asked Amanda, deciding to play dumb.

"Well, Tyler Hudson is a nice enough man, but his strengths lie more in the area of handling animal complaints or disputes between neighbors. Suspicious death is a little out of his territory."

"I thought the state police usually handled that stuff."

"Yes. But the local authorities don't have to ask them in to investigate unless it's obviously a crime. I'm not sure that Tyler believes Hazel's death was anything but an accident. Plus, the state guys have their plates pretty full right now with the girl missing." Susan's face grew very somber as she came to the end of the sentence.

"Do you know Anne Martin?"

Susan nodded her head and her lips trembled as she spoke. "She worked here part-time shelving books. She was a smart, attractive young woman. I really hope nothing has happened to her, but I can't imagine why she would have disappeared. She was very responsible."

Amanda nodded and changed the topic. "I was wondering whether you and Professor Wilmot ever had a conversation about the ghost in the Shadsborough Inn."

Susan stared at the countertop.

"Actually, we did, and I was the one doing most of the talking. I was telling her how I felt kind of responsible for the entire thing."

"How do you mean?" Amanda asked, surprised.

"Well, we have an elementary school here in town, and part of my job is to go into every class once a month and read them an age-appropriate story. A few days before the boys saw the crying girl at the inn, I was in their fifth-grade class, and I read them a simplified version of the Washington Irving story, *The Legend of Sleepy Hollow*. I thought they would enjoy it during the Halloween season. It's always hard to find stories that the boys will listen to."

"I'll bet they loved it, with the headless horseman and all that sort of thing," said Amanda.

"They did. But after I was finished, I made a mistake. I asked them if anyone knew of any local legends."

"Seems like a harmless-enough question."

"Not really." Susan smiled. "When you're in the classroom, you have to be like a lawyer in the courtroom;

never ask a question that you don't already know the answer to, or else you may get an unpleasant surprise."

"And that's what happened this time?"

Susan nodded. "Jimmy Racine brought up this story about the ghost of a crying girl in the Shadsborough Inn. He and some of his friends seemed to get excited about the idea of finding out if the ghost was still there because they walk past the place on a regular basis at night. I tried to discourage them, but I left the classroom with a bad feeling that they weren't going to take my advice."

"Did Jimmy say where he had heard this story?"

"All he would say is that someone had told him this story about a girl who had been murdered there and had claimed that it was true."

"You'd never heard this story before?"

She shook her head. "At first I just figured that it was the kind of story that an old abandoned house would provoke in a kid's imagination, and that Jimmy was exaggerating a bit by saying that someone had told it to him. However, the librarian in a village is sort of the unofficial historian, so I did some research. We don't have a large reference department, but we do have more than our share of books on the history of the local area. I found an account of the story in a book written in the late nineteenth century by a man who retired to the village after teaching history at Harvard for much of his life. It was kind of an autobiography and description of what life was like in rural New Hampshire at the time."

"Was that when this girl supposedly was killed?"

"Oh, no. The story was already old by then. According to Harold Collins, the man who wrote this book, the murder happened in 1836 when the inn was a busy stagecoach stopping point. The girl was Charity

O'Neil. Her parents, Wallace and Mary O'Neil, owned the inn."

"How did the girl come to be murdered?"

"No one was certain that it really was a murder. The story got started because she waited tables and was seen spending a great deal of time one night talking and laughing with a stranger who had been passing through on horseback. In the morning, the man had disappeared and Charity's body was found at the foot of the cellar stairs."

"Just like Professor Wilmot's."

Susan nodded. "But in this case people suspected that perhaps Charity and this man had agreed to meet in the kitchen after everyone else had gone to bed for a little 'dalliance,' as people put it in those days. Charity had a bit of a reputation as a girl who liked men. We'll never know for sure, but some people figured that things got out of hand and this stranger killed her."

"He was never identified or apprehended?"

"People didn't inquire as carefully about a traveler's name in those days. And although the local marshal at the time searched up and down the road, there was never a clue as to where the man had gone."

"When did the ghost story begin?"

"Less than a year later. Mary O'Neil was a high-strung woman from all accounts, and she was the first one to hear the sobbing coming from the basement. One of the maids claimed to hear it as well, but she may just have been supporting her mistress. Over the next twenty years there were periodic reports by guests and people who worked at the inn that they had heard crying in the basement."

"Any reported sightings of a ghost?"

The librarian shook her head. "That's what makes this case so strange. Jimmy said that he definitely saw a girl."

"Possibly Anne Martin?"

Susan frowned. "She was covered in a veil and wearing a long white nightgown, according to Jimmy's description. He couldn't see her face."

"Would he have recognized Anne if he saw her?"

"I think so. Jimmy used to come into the library after school sometimes. He likes to read. But I can't imagine that Anne would get involved in some kind of silly prank like that. She was high-spirited, but not stupid. I find it hard to believe that her disappearance has anything to do with what Jimmy saw."

"So you think he really did see a ghost?"

Susan smiled. "I don't believe in ghosts any more than you do, I imagine. No, if he didn't make it up, then I think he saw someone. I just can't believe that it was Anne."

Amanda paused. The morning light was starting to move around to the side of the building, leaving the room where they were standing suddenly darker and more shadowy. The mountain was visible through the window that was just over Susan's shoulder. Amanda stared at it for a moment like it was another person in the room. Susan caught her glance.

"Yeah, it is kind of spooky, isn't it? Even though I've been employed here almost three years, sometimes I'll be working and suddenly get the feeling that the mountain is watching me through the window like something alive."

"What's the name of the mountain?"

"Lost Trail Mountain."

"Like Pat Bennett's inn."

Susan nodded. "There's a story behind that too. The name is a rough translation of what the Native Americans who lived around here called it. Apparently, long before the Europeans came here, a large hunting party once followed a trail up the mountain in search of game and was never seen again."

"Between the inn and the mountain, it sounds like Shadsborough has more than its share of spooky happenings. Were you raised around here?"

Susan laughed. "Not likely. I moved here from Chicago four years ago with my then-husband, who was all excited about the benefits of living off the land. That lasted about six months, until he discovered how hard the land can be and took off."

"But you stayed."

"There were debts to be paid, and by the time that was done, I had this job and had settled in here."

"What about Anne Martin's disappearance?" Amanda asked. "Do you think there was foul play there?"

"At first I kept hoping that she just had a wild, crazy moment and ran off somewhere with a friend. But now . . . I just don't know."

The door opened and closed behind Amanda, but she didn't turn around. Susan rolled her eyes in warning, but Amanda missed the hint and continued speaking.

"Do you know why Hazel was so upset by what the boys saw at the inn?"

"Probably because like every other fool person in this town, she thought the place was haunted," an angry voice said behind her.

Amanda spun around. The man standing behind her looked to be in his fifties, but it was difficult to tell. A plaid hunter's cap was pulled down almost to his ears, and his pale, chubby face, which almost seemed to be formed out of dough, made him look like a very old baby. The only sign of animation on his face were his eyes, which at the moment were a blazing, bloodshot blue. Behind him stood a tall, shy-acting man in his early thirties with dark hair and concerned brown eyes who appeared rather embarrassed by the older man's behavior.

"This is John Phelps and his son, Michael. The Phelps family has owned the Shadsborough Inn for two generations," Susan said.

"Mr. Phelps." Amanda put out her hand to the man, but he ignored it.

"And it's bad enough that folks in town believe that crazy story that was long forgotten, even in my grandfather's time. Now outsiders are coming in and rooting around. What are you, some kind of reporter?"

His comment was close enough to the truth that Amanda blushed slightly. "I was a friend of Hazel Wilmot's."

"Well, she's dead," John Phelps said. "Broke her fool neck trespassing on my property."

A worried look came into the man's eyes. "Now her son's in town wanting to know how his mother got into the inn, and my insurance company is telling me that I should have secured the abandoned property better. How am I supposed to do any better? All the doors were locked. I don't know how those kids got inside in the first place. And I put new locks on the doors the day after I heard about them going down in the cellar. So I sure don't know how that crazy old lady got in there."

"I'm sure no one blames you," Susan said soothingly.

"They better not," the man snapped, then he suddenly seemed tired. His body slumped, and his son reached out to take his arm. "All I ever wanted to do was see the inn running again," the older man said mournfully. "I was so close. Now that will never happen."

"Why don't we go home now, Dad?" His son took his

arm and ineffectually tried to turn him toward the door, but the man spun back toward Amanda.

"There's no story here, lady, so why don't you get out of town?" He raised a hand that would have been threatening but for the obvious trembling and the fact that he was already slumping backward into his son's arms.

Michael Phelps gave Susan and Amanda an apologetic look. "Let's go home, Dad. You need to have a little rest." While the women watched, he helped his father across the library and out the door.

"What's wrong with him?" Amanda asked once the door closed.

"Cancer. I've heard that he only has a few more months to live."

"How sad. What did he mean when he said that he was close to getting the inn running again?"

Susan smiled. "It's been a kind of pipe dream with John to reopen the inn. I've heard that his father wanted to do it and passed the idea on to his son. But that was just about the only inheritance he got, aside from a hundred acres of land around the inn and a small farm outside of town."

"So he never had the money to restore the place?"

"Have you seen it?"

"Just passed by on the road," Amanda answered cautiously.

"Well, it would take a small fortune to fix it up, and John's never had much money. He did a little farming for a while. Then he ran a roofing business. Oh, he did well enough to make ends meet, but he was never able to put aside the kind of cash you'd need to get the inn going again." Susan paused for a moment as though wondering how much to tell Amanda. "Actually, I don't think he was ever quite as obsessed by the whole thing until after Marsha, his wife, died four years ago. He married rather late in life, and losing her seemed to tip him over the edge into almost a fantasy world."

"But he did seem to say that the inn was almost ready to reopen," said Amanda.

Susan shrugged. "John was talking for a while about a couple down in Concord being interested in buying the inn and all the land around it. But how close that was to actually happening is hard to tell. Between his wife's death and all the medication he's on, you just don't know how much of what he tells you is real and how much is imaginary."

"His son seems worried about him," Amanda said.

"Stepson. Marsha had been married before. She was a smart, attractive woman. I didn't know her well because she died shortly after I came to Shadsborough, but everyone says that she was the real center of the family, handled the books for the roofing company and made all the major decisions. Without her John is really lost."

"And now he's dying."

Susan nodded sadly. "It really goes to show that sometimes life isn't fair. It's a shame about John, and it was too bad that Hazel had to die in that stupid accident."

Amanda nodded. "Are the stairs in the inn really that dangerous?"

"I've never been in the place. You'd have to ask Chief Hudson." She paused for a moment. "Of course, you could sneak in there and take a look for yourself, I suppose."

Amanda worked at looking innocent. "Isn't the inn sealed up?"

"Sure. But some kids got in last night, I hear. Good thing it was last night and not tonight."

"Why's that?"

"Well, according to what I've read, people only hear the crying on Mondays, Wednesdays, and Saturdays. And don't ask me why, because I have no idea."

"So the ghost should cry tonight," Amanda said with a faint, skeptical smile.

Susan smiled back with the same degree of skepticism. "If you believe that kind of thing."

Chapter Eight

Y ou want to go back to the inn tonight because the ghost will be there. Did I hear you right?" Marcie asked in a tone that suggested Amanda had lost her reason. "I thought you didn't believe in that supernatural stuff."

They were sitting in the parlor of the Lost Trail Inn. It was too early for lunch, but Pat Bennett had provided them with tea and muffins. Amanda had restricted herself to the tea, but Marcie had eaten a corn muffin and was already eyeing a second muffin with blue dots, which suggested it might have blueberries in it.

"I'm not expecting a real ghost. But I hope that the person who attacked Professor Wilmot will be there again."

"Why would he or she return?"

"I don't know, but Jimmy saw the ghost on Monday and the professor died at the inn on Saturday. So there does seem to be a pattern."

"So what about last Monday? That's the night we think that Arthur Wilmot was there. He didn't say anything about seeing a ghost."

"He didn't tell us much of anything," Amanda pointed out. "That's why we're going to pay him a visit."

Marcie frowned and reached for the other muffin.

"What's wrong?" Amanda asked.

Marcie took her time taking the paper off the muffin, then tore off a small piece and chewed it carefully. "Nothing," she finally answered. "It's just that I think we're too focused on the inn. I think we ought to be asking ourselves what motive someone might have for murdering Professor Wilmot, if she was murdered."

"Do you have anyone in mind?"

"What about Middie Ross? Professor Wilmot virtually accused her of having something to do with the ghost at the inn."

Amanda looked across the room, watching the sun make patterns on the gleaming hardwood floors. "If we're going to talk about motives, why would Middie Ross want people to think that the inn was haunted?"

"Maybe she wanted to drum up business," Marcie suggested.

"You mean she's offering an herbal cure for seeing ghosts?" Amanda asked with a faint smile.

"What if she was trying to get converts to her religion? Or maybe she thought that getting a local ghost story in the newspapers would get her some publicity. Lots of people just want to be famous."

"Maybe you're right," Amanda said, trying to be conciliatory. "We really haven't any idea why someone would be haunting the inn."

Marcie took another bite of muffin and nodded her head vigorously. "The one thing we do know so far is that this ghost story is hurting John Phelps' chances for selling the inn. Could Phelps have an enemy who wants to keep him from selling the inn?"

Amanda nodded. "That's the problem here. All we have is speculation. We don't know the village well enough to figure out what people's motives might be."

Amanda was about to say more when loud voices from the hallway made her stop. Pat Bennett seemed to be protesting to some man with a gravelly voice. The voices grew closer, and a moment later a large, florid man wearing a police uniform burst into the parlor with Pat close behind, looking as though she wanted to physically restrain him. He marched over to where Marcie and Amanda were sitting. Amanda immediately got to her feet so as not to give him the advantage of looking down on her.

"I want to know what the two of you are doing in Shadsborough," he demanded, then paused to catch his breath.

"This is Tyler Hudson, the chief of police," Pat said.

"Pleased to meet you, Chief," Amanda said, putting out her hand. "I'm Amanda Vickers, we spoke on the phone about Hazel Wilmot. This is my friend Marcie Ducasse."

The chief reluctantly took her outstretched hand, politeness winning out briefly over his anger.

"You're the reporter," he said accusingly, as if that were a punishable offense.

"Editor, actually," Amanda replied with a cool smile.

"So what are you doing here in town? I told you that there was nothing more to find out about the Wilmot woman's death."

"I thought I owed it to her to find out what happened," Amanda replied.

"So you and your friend come here and start wandering around town asking people questions. You should have come to me first."

"And what would you have told me?"

"The same thing I told you over the phone. Hazel Wilmot slipped on the cellar stairs and fell."

"That's what I thought," Amanda said, staring hard at the chief.

His face turned red. "What's that supposed to mean?"

The woman shrugged. "Nothing. But it seems to me that since you have a boy seeing ghosts in an abandoned inn, an old woman falling in the same place, and a young girl missing, you might make more of an effort to tie them all together."

Chief Hudson snorted his contempt. "That's the trouble with you amateurs. You want to make up a good story, so you take a bunch of coincidences and string them together."

"And you want to keep thinking this is a nice quiet town, so you ignore the obvious connections between events," Amanda shot back.

He squinted hard at her and his eyes became small. Amanda knew that she shouldn't have provoked him. The chief of police in a small town is a little god who can do virtually whatever he wants.

"And I'm telling you that if I hear from one more person that you've been going around asking questions, I'll bring you in for harassment."

"I'm not harassing anyone, Chief, I'm just asking questions in order to get information."

"I'm the one who asks questions in this village, not some outsider just looking to stir things up. I'll bet you didn't even know Hazel Wilmot."

Out of the corner of her eye, Amanda saw that Marcie was opening her mouth to make an angry retort. Amanda made a small silencing gesture. There was no reason for both of them to get into trouble.

"Do *you* want to say something?" Chief Hudson asked, staring at the younger woman. "I'd just love to have an excuse to take the both of you in for questioning."

"That's enough, Chief," Pat Bennett said in a surprisingly firm voice.

Hudson looked over at her like he wouldn't mind running her out of town as well. Then his expression changed as he remembered that she wasn't an outsider, but a respected member of the community who ran an important business in town. Reluctantly, he nodded.

"Okay," he agreed, "that's enough *for now.*"

He turned away from the women and headed toward the door, then he stopped and looked back at Amanda and Marcie. Amanda guessed that it was mostly for effect. "Remember, you've been warned."

"We'll remember, Chief," Amanda said in a cheerful voice.

Her cheerfulness seemed to annoy the chief even more. Without another word, he stomped out into the hall and left.

"Talk about rude," Marcie said when she heard the door close.

"Tyler isn't really a bad man," Pat Bennett said, "but he's not accustomed to dealing with folks from outside the town. Plus things have been moving too fast for him lately. Hazel's death, then the state police searching for Anne: all of this has gotten him on edge."

"Thanks for running interference for us with the chief," Marcie said.

"You should have told me you were reporters," the

woman said with asperity. She turned stiffly and began to walk out of the room.

"Wait!" Amanda said. "We aren't reporters."

Pat turned back, her face red with anger. "Do you work for a magazine?"

"Yes, like I told the chief, we're editors," Amanda admitted.

"Did you even know Hazel?"

"Yes. Everything I said to you about that is true."

The woman paused. "You should have told me about your jobs."

Amanda nodded. "You're right. But at first we didn't know you or how you would react to having us in town. We didn't want everyone to know that we worked for a magazine or else they'd never talk to us."

"And after you got to know me, you still didn't think that I could be trusted?"

Amanda paused for a moment not sure how to say that she didn't trust anybody without offending the woman. Marcie stepped in quickly to fill the gap.

"Of course we trusted you," Marcie said, "but we knew that eventually it would get out that we worked for a magazine. We didn't want you to have to lie when the other folks in the village came to you and asked if you knew about our jobs. We figured this way you wouldn't get in trouble with your neighbors."

Pat Bennett studied Marcie's face for a moment as if trying to ascertain whether she was telling the truth. Finally she nodded and gave her a faint smile.

"If that's the case, then I guess I have to say that I appreciate your sensitivity to my situation. However, now it will be all over town that the two of you are reporters. What am I supposed to do?"

"Maybe we should leave," Marcie suggested, glancing at Amanda. "After all, we can find somewhere to stay outside of town and drive in to ask our questions."

Amanda nodded reluctantly.

"The nearest place to stay is back near the highway. That's over a half-hour away," Pat Bennett said.

"Difficult but not impossible," Amanda said, standing up and turning to Marcie. "I think we should go get packed."

"No, no, stay here," Pat said wearily, waving them back down. "Hazel was my friend, and if something criminal happened to her in that cellar, I don't want Tyler Hudson or anyone else covering it up."

"Are you sure?" Marcie asked.

Pat nodded. "Just because I live in this town doesn't mean that I have to do what the majority want me to do. Sometimes you have to go your own way."

"Good for you," Marcie said, flashing her a smile.

The woman gave her a curt nod and left the room.

"You did all right there," Amanda said softly. "Your comment about our not telling her the truth about our jobs being for her own good really turned the tide."

"That was the truth."

Amanda looked puzzled.

"Oh, I know you deceived her because you're a hard-bitten reporter and don't trust anyone. But I did it because I thought it would give her some cover with her neighbors."

"You *really* thought about that?" asked Amanda.

"Sure. I care about other people."

"So do I," Amanda replied, stung.

"But you care about the job more."

Amanda frowned, but didn't respond.

Chapter Nine

When they pulled up in front of Arthur Wilmot's house, he was standing in the driveway facing the open trunk of his car. A suitcase and an armful of clothes were on the asphalt next to him. As they walked up the drive, he turned to look at them. Then he spun around quickly and threw the suitcase into the trunk. He tossed the clothes in after it.

"Making a fast escape, Artie?" Marcie asked.

Arthur spun around again and almost fell backward into the trunk.

"Is there anything wrong?" Amanda asked.

"No, of course not," he said. "I've decided that there's nothing more I can do here in Shadsborough."

"Really?" Marcie said in a tone of utter disbelief.

He nodded nervously. "I've arranged for my mother's body to be shipped back to Chicago for burial. Once the will is settled, I'll see about selling the house. I'm going home. I've got a job to get back to."

Marcie looked over at Amanda. "What do you think?"

Sensing that Marcie wanted to take control of the conversation, Amanda shrugged noncommittally.

"Well, I'll tell you what I think. I think we have a guy here who was really anxious last night to find out what happened to his mother but today seems to have changed his mind. That makes me wonder what happened between last night and right now." She stared hard at the man. "What did happen, Arthur?"

He started to open his mouth, obviously planning to deny the occurrence of anything unusual. Then he paused and licked his lips.

"Let's go inside. I'm not comfortable standing out here on the street."

He shut the trunk and they trooped up on the porch and into the living room of the bungalow.

When the two women were settled on the couch facing Arthur, who was squirming uncomfortably in a wooden rocker, Marcie asked again, "What happened?"

"I got a phone call."

"When?" Amanda asked.

"This morning. Not more than an hour ago."

"What did the caller say?" Amanda asked patiently.

"He said that unless I wanted the same thing to happen to me that happened to my mother I should leave town right away."

"It was a man's voice?"

Arthur nodded. "I think so, but it was kind of muffled. Like he was trying to conceal his identity."

"Who have you spoken to since you've been in town?" Amanda asked.

"Well, I went right to the police station as soon as I arrived. I talked to the chief and one of the deputies to see what they could tell me about my mother's accident.

All they did was tell me the story about this ghost business and ask me why my mother would have been searching the inn."

"You didn't know?"

He shook his head. "I hadn't spoken with my mother in almost a month. I had no idea what she thought she would find there."

"Did you talk to anyone else in town?"

"After seeing the police, I went to the grocery store to pick up a few things. I recognized a couple of people that I'd met on previous visits."

"Is that it?"

"When I was coming out of the store, this weird old guy who had been in the police station came up to me and said that my mother had been trespassing on his property when she died. He said that if I had any plans to sue him, I'd better forget it because she had no right to be there. Then he went on about the ghost story and claimed my mother was one of the people who had been spreading it around town."

Amanda described John Phelps.

"That sounds like the guy," Arthur said. "There was a younger man with him."

"Probably his stepson, Michael Phelps."

"He tried to pull the old guy away from me and quiet him down. But he wouldn't listen."

"Like any small town, gossip travels like wildfire," said Amanda. "I'll bet that everyone knows by now that you're in town. There's no way we're going to figure out who made that call."

Arthur nodded sadly. "That's why I figured that I should just leave."

"So all that talk last night really didn't mean anything,"

said Marcie. "You really don't care whether we discover what happened to your mother."

"Of course, I care," Arthur shot back, "but I don't see any way of finding out. This is a weird little place. An outsider hasn't got a chance of proving what happened."

"So you plan to just give up and leave, Arthur. Is that the kind of son you are?"

Looking like he'd been slapped, Arthur began to get out of the chair. Fearing that he was going to throw them out of the house, Amanda said, "You did search the inn on Monday when you first arrived, didn't you?"

The man paused, then sank back into the chair.

"Yeah. After I went to the police station and got no satisfaction, I came here and waited until after dark. Then I took the crowbar from the garage and went out to the inn. I pried the boards off the front door. I put them back in place loosely so no one would know that I had broken in. Then I headed straight for the cellar to see if there was anything the police had missed."

"Was there?" Amanda asked. She held her breath hoping to get an affirmative answer.

Arthur reached in the pocket of his pants and took out a gold chain. He reached forward and handed it across to Amanda. It was a bracelet: *From George to Hazel: With Love* was engraved on it.

"Your mother's bracelet?" Marcie asked.

"Actually, it's an ankle bracelet," the man said with a slight blush. "My father gave it to my mother when they were first married. I don't think I've ever known her not to wear it."

"The clasp seems to be bent," Amanda said, examining it. "As if it had been pulled off rather than removed."

Amanda continued staring at the bracelet, trying to

imagine the Hazel Wilmot she knew wearing such a piece of jewelry. She reminded herself that everyone was young once and that some people didn't show their emotions as readily as others. *I should know,* she thought.

"Which ankle did she wear it on?" asked Marcie.

"Always her left."

"And where did you find it?"

"On the floor in the cellar."

"I'm surprised that the police didn't spot it," Amanda commented.

"It was way back in a corner. I almost didn't find it myself. Half the cellar is filled with boxes of old stuff that they used to use when the place was an inn."

"Did you discover anything else?"

Arthur cleared his throat. "I had to leave in a hurry."

"Why?" Marcie asked.

The man looked down at his feet as though about to say something he'd rather not.

"I heard a noise, and I ran away."

"A noise?" Amanda asked.

"I heard footsteps in the upstairs hall. It sounded as if they were heading into the kitchen. I thought that some-one might be coming towards the cellar, so I decided to take off."

"How did you get out?' Marcie asked. "You didn't go back upstairs?"

"No, I was afraid that I would run into whoever was up there. I took the stairs that go directly outside from the basement."

"They were unlocked?" asked Marcie.

"They lock from the inside. You just pull back a latch and they open."

"Did you leave them unlocked when you left?"

"Sure. There's no way to lock them from the outside. Anyway, I just closed the door and ran. I didn't want whoever was up there to see me."

Marcie glanced over at Amanda. Amanda knew that she was wondering why the way down into the cellar had been locked last night if Arthur had left it open the night before.

"Why didn't you go back in through the cellar door last night instead of using the front door?" asked Marcie.

The man shrugged. "I was a little nervous about going back down in the cellar, so I figured I'd check out the upstairs first to make sure no one was around."

"And the boards were still in place at the front door the way you had left them."

Wilmot nodded.

"I wonder how the person you heard upstairs that night got into the house without removing the boards."

"Maybe he put them back the same way Arthur did," Marcie suggested.

Amanda nodded, then turned back to Arthur. "And why did you attack me?"

"I thought that you knew something about what had happened to my mother."

"And you rushed right ahead and tackled me, even though you'd run away the night before."

Arthur smiled sheepishly. "You didn't look really tough."

Marcie grinned but hid it quickly. Then she put on a hard expression and leaned forward on the sofa toward Arthur as if only an invisible wire kept her from leaping across the center of the living room and knocking some sense into him.

"So now you're planning to run away again because

you got a scary phone call?" Marcie said with a sign-song of sarcasm in her voice.

"Well, wouldn't you?"

"She wasn't my mother."

The man sank back in the chair.

"You gave us a good line last night about how much you wanted to discover the truth about your mother's death. Now the first crank phone call sends you scurrying off with your tail between your legs."

"I want to stay," he pleaded, "but I've got my own life to think about."

"Maybe there could be a compromise here," Amanda suggested.

Arthur turned to her with a desperate hopefulness in his eyes.

"What if you left this house, but got a room in a motel out near the highway? Then whoever called would think that you'd left, but you'd still be nearby in case we needed help."

Arthur thought about it for a moment, then nodded his head. "I could stay for a few more days if you really need my help."

"We do," Amanda said fervently.

He visibly straightened up in the chair and nodded his agreement. Some of his cockiness seemed to return at the thought that these women needed him. Amanda had to restrain herself from adding that the word *need* was being defined very loosely here. Instead, she smiled her gratitude. "I think it would be very helpful to have an ally that the enemy doesn't know about."

Marcie had a disgusted look on her face, and Amanda gave her a warning glance not to say anything.

Amanda wrote down her cell phone number and handed it to him. "Do you have a cell phone?" she asked.

Arthur nodded, and they exchanged numbers.

"And you'll keep me updated on your progress?" he asked.

"Of course."

The man gave her a curt nod, suddenly taking on the role of a commander dismissing the troops.

"What a jerk!" Marcie said when they were back in the car. "Do we really need him hanging around? Maybe it would be better if he did go back home."

"I'm not sure whether he'll prove useful or not, but I like the idea of having someone around for support that the rest of the people in this town don't know about. It might prove helpful."

"Are we still going back to the inn tonight?" Marcie asked.

"That's right."

Marcie remained silent for a long moment. "So what are we going to do this afternoon?"

Amanda looked up the street at Lost Trail Mountain filling most of the horizon in front of them.

"I'm getting sick of this place. How about we go down to Concord and look around? Maybe we can do some shopping and find a nice restaurant for lunch."

Marcie smiled. "I thought you'd never ask."

Chapter Ten

So you think buying that dress was a good idea?" Marcie asked for what seemed to Amanda to be the tenth time.

"Yes. Now that you're going to be out in the field more, you never know when a dress might come in handy. Even today some events really require that you wear one."

"I never had a dress in college. I even went to my job interviews wearing slacks."

Amanda well remembered the interview of two months ago when Marcie had showed up in the middle of August wearing a pair of rather shiny corduroys with a long-sleeved blouse. She was tempted to tell her that it had been her fine grades and glowing letters of recommendation that got her the job, not her taste in fashion.

"Well, it's time to make the transition from being a student to being a career woman," Amanda replied.

"I suppose."

They had spent the afternoon walking around Concord, stopping in the small shops and generally enjoying a beautiful day with no obligations. Amanda had to admit that not seeing Lost Trail Mountain hovering in the distance gave her a sense of relief, like finally being out from under an enemy's watchful gaze. At first she had wondered what they would do all afternoon, but when Marcie stopped to stare at a dress hanging in the window of a boutique, Amanda made it her mission to see that her colleague had at least one decent outfit to wear. Having only older brothers, Amanda wondered whether this was what it felt like to have a younger sister, and not for the first time, she thought that having another female in the family other than her mother would have been a good thing.

After having a late lunch, they turned their attention to bookstores, where they were both surprised to find that they shared an interest in mysteries and historical fiction. When the sun showed signs of setting, they purchased an overstuffed turkey sandwich to split and a couple of sodas to take with them. Amanda had told Pat Bennett that they wouldn't be back until the evening, so they hadn't returned to their rooms but had gone directly to the Shadsborough Inn, finding a place to park off the road near where Arthur Wilmot's car had been concealed. Now they were eating and watching the darkness gradually deepen.

"I suppose my not having a dress gives you some idea of how exciting my social life was in college," Marcie said.

"College events are usually pretty informal," Amanda replied, not sure how much she wanted to hear about Marcie's past.

"Most of my events were just a few friends going out to a movie."

"No guys?"

Marcie gave a hoarse laugh. "I scared them off. Between my dedication to sports and my focus on good grades, I think most of them figured that either I wouldn't know how to have fun or that I'd hurt them."

"A lot of college guys can be immature."

"Yeah. But they were probably right. I was kind of career driven. When you've spent most of your life living on some Army base where all you can see are sky and open spaces, you get the feeling that things are passing you by. I figured that getting to go to college in Boston was a chance to find out what real life is like. Once I saw it, I wanted to make sure that I never had to go back to the little corner of the world where I started. I had to do well enough to have a career that would amount to something and not end up like most of the kids I knew from back home."

"I see what you mean."

"So maybe I'm not exactly a well-rounded person," Marcie added with a hint of humor in her voice.

"Maybe being well rounded is overrated," said Amanda, noisily balling up her sandwich wrapper and finishing her soda.

Taking that as an indication that she should change the subject, Marcie asked, "Did you call Greg today?"

"I called him back at the restaurant when you were in the ladies' room."

"Did you tell him what we were up to tonight?"

"No," Amanda admitted, feeling a surge of guilt at the fact that she was concealing stuff from Greg.

"Afraid he'd tell us not to go?"

"Were you hoping that he would?" Amanda replied sharply.

"I'm ready to go," Marcie said, clearly stung by the

criticism. "But I'd just like to know that all this is on the up and up."

"Don't worry about it," Amanda said. "Greg lets me make my own decisions under circumstances like this. Now let's get changed."

"Sure, whatever you say," Marcie responded, clearly not convinced that they were doing the right thing.

Amanda had suggested that they bring along jeans and heavy sweaters to wear under their light jackets. Marcie had asked why they didn't just dress that way before leaving the inn. Amanda knew that her comment that she didn't want Pat to suspect what they were up to had made her seem paranoid to Marcie, but she truly didn't know who to trust in Shadsborough and wasn't about to give anyone a chance to anticipate their plans.

So now the two women stood on opposite sides of the car, trying to keep their sock feet off the ground as much as possible, and changed into their warmer clothes. When they were finished, Amanda walked the ten feet or so to the road and looked back to see if the car was visible. Headlights flashed past, and Amanda crouched down, keeping her eyes on her car to see if the passing beams revealed anything of their location.

"Is it hidden enough?" Marcie asked when she returned.

"Pretty well. There was a little flash of color when the headlights hit it, but I think someone would have to be really paying attention to notice anything. Hopefully we won't be here very long."

After locking the car and making sure that they had their flashlights, the women walked along the side of the road toward the inn, leaping back into the undergrowth on the rare occasions when a car drove by. In about five minutes, they were standing at the top of the driveway looking down into the darkness that enveloped the inn.

"Should we go around back again?" asked Marcie.

"Let's save ourselves the effort and give the front door a try."

"Don't you think the police will have boarded it up again or padlocked it after chasing us off last night?" Marcie asked.

"I've given up trying to guess what the police in this town will do and not do."

Staying in the deeper shadows as much as possible, they went down the driveway toward the front door.

"Even though this is a Wednesday night, you really can't think that whoever was playing ghost will really come back again after everything that's happened?" asked Marcie.

"I'd be very surprised."

"So why are we here?"

"Just to make sure. Plus, I want to check out the basement. Arthur left in a hurry. He said so himself. That means that there still might be some clues lying around as to who's behind all this. And I'd just like to have a look around to get a sense of the place where Professor Wilmot died."

By now they had reached the front porch. The beam of light that Amanda flashed over the front door revealed that it was boarded up.

"I guess that's that," Marcie said, preparing to walk around to the back of the inn. "We should have brought a crowbar."

"Wait." Amanda handed Marcie her flashlight. She then reached out and pulled on one of the boards. After a couple of tugs, it came away from the frame of the door with a loud squeak.

"Either you're stronger than I think you are or someone loosened those boards again just like the other night."

"But this time I don't think we can blame Arthur Wilmot. The police must have secured this door last night or this morning. Since then someone has been back inside."

"I wonder who," Marcie said.

"Well, I don't think ghosts go around with crowbars."

"Very funny."

"At least we know that whoever was inside must have left and put the boards back in place so the police wouldn't get suspicious."

"So you think that means it's safe to go inside?"

"I *think* so."

"I was hoping for a more definite answer than that."

Amanda laughed softly and began tugging at the other two boards. With Marcie's help they soon had the front door open. Amanda shined her flashlight down the long hall. The door to the kitchen at the end of the hall was closed.

"Ready to go?" she asked Marcie.

"We're just going right down the hall and into the cellar. We look around for clues, then come out again."

"You've got it."

There was a long silence.

"Okay, I'm ready."

Amanda led the way. When she was a few feet down the hallway, she checked the rooms to the left and right just to see if anything had changed. They looked exactly the same as last night, empty of furniture and appearing rather forlorn. Amanda continued walking, pausing briefly with every other step to listen to the house.

"What's the matter?" Marcie asked softly the second time she paused.

"I'm trying to hear if there are any strange sounds."

Marcie made a snorting noise. "In my opinion, there's nothing but strange sounds in this place: the floors creak, the walls groan, and the windows seem to get brushed every five seconds by a bush or tree that rattles like a skeleton. Why don't we just move as fast as possible and get this thing done?"

Amanda walked more quickly but she came to a stop when they reached the closed door into the kitchen. She expected to hear Marcie say "Now what!" but there was only silence behind her. *Maybe Marcie is hoping that I change my mind and decide that we don't really have to check out the cellar,* Amanda thought, smiling to herself. She reached forward and pushed open the door into the kitchen. Despite her common sense telling her that the house was most likely empty, she half-expected someone to jump out at her, but all she saw in the glow of her flashlight was the large, silent, empty kitchen. The utter stillness of the room seemed to mock her exaggerated expectations.

Marcie remained quiet. Only her fast breathing told Amanda that she was right behind her. Amanda moved forward across the width of the room to the door to the cellar. It was closed. Not pausing this time, she quickly pushed the door open.

Three things struck Amanda simultaneously as she stood at the top of the stairs: a cool breeze smelling of vegetation was wafting up the steps, a light was glowing dimly somewhere in the cellar, and a woman was softly crying. Marcie's breathing suddenly stopped.

"What's going on here?" Marcie asked a second later

in the ragged tone of someone who really didn't want to know the answer.

"I'm going down to find out. You wait up here."

"Are you sure?"

"I want you to make sure that whoever is down there doesn't get past me and escape."

"Can we handle what's down there?" Marcie asked doubtfully.

Amanda paused for a moment. A very good question. Just the kind of question she would normally have posed herself. Even if she didn't believe that whatever was down there had any supernatural powers, it could still be a dangerous human being. *I've never believed in taking unnecessary risks. Why am I so willing to do it now?* she asked herself. The answer that came back to her was clear and compelling. *When my father needed me, I wasn't there. I wasn't there for Hazel when she called. This time I'm going to be there.*

Amanda was halfway down the stairs when she heard a muffled cry. She turned back just in time to see the cellar door slam shut. Amanda raced back up the stairs and tried to pull it open, but it was locked. She could hear scraping noises on the other side as if someone was being dragged away. *Something is happening to Marcie,* she thought, pulling even more desperately on the doorknob.

"Marcie!" she shouted but got no answer.

A sudden cold certainty came over Amanda, and she stopped banging on the door. *The only way to help Marcie is to keep going straight ahead, then I can go out through the cellar door,* she told herself. *Only by facing whatever is in the basement can I save her.*

Amanda started back down the stairs, taking each step cautiously, not wanting to be taken by surprise by whatever was down there. When her shoes scraped on the rough stone and dirt floor, she directed the flashlight toward the glow coming from the other side of the cellar.

Sheer draperies of some sort had been arranged like hospital curtains across one end of the cellar. They blew gently in the breeze coming through the open cellar hatchway. Through them Amanda could make out the silhouette of a woman who was sitting over what appeared to be a flickering candle. Her posture was bent as if she were in pain or staring down at something. The low sobbing had a deeply personal quality and gave the impression that the woman had no idea that anyone else was present and was completely lost in a moment of private grief. As Amanda slowly walked toward the figure, the crying stopped.

"Get back!" the woman shrieked.

Amanda froze. Shocked by the sound of the voice and the fact that the woman apparently knew she was there.

"Get back, murderer. You are no better than he was."

Confused, Amanda took a tentative step forward. The shadow behind the curtain straightened and turned toward Amanda.

"Indeed, you are worse. Men have killed women from the beginning of time, but what kind of daughter allows her own father to die? To die by fire is surely the most painful of ways to leave this earth."

Amanda stopped breathing. She dropped the flashlight and her hands clenched at her chest.

Who was this woman who knew her innermost secrets? Who could make these accusations that she had only dared make to herself on those first long sleepless nights after her father's death? Perhaps she really was a ghost.

"Who are you?"

"A victim of one who was as cruel as yourself. One who killed someone he claimed to love. Be gone from here, before you are judged and condemned to spend eternity in torment as he does."

"You don't understand," Amanda said.

"I understand all too well," the woman replied in a voice that ended in a broken sob. "All too well."

"But why are you here?" Amanda asked softly.

"I am here to warn you to stay away from this place. Stay away or else you will pay the same price as my murderer."

Suddenly, the candle went out, plunging the cellar into darkness except for the beam of the flashlight that was lying on the floor. Amanda stood still, trying to hear what was happening in the darkness. There was the scurrying of feet followed by silence. After taking several deep breaths, Amanda finally felt able to move. She picked up the flashlight, thankful that some light was available to help her to find her way out of the cellar. She slowly approached the curtains and pulled them aside. On the other side was a simple wooden stool next to a battered table. Both looked like they might have been taken from another part of the house. A plain white candle stood in the middle of the table in a pool of its own slowly hardening wax.

Amanda directed the flashlight around the basement. In front of her were concrete steps leading up through the hatchway to the outside, the same way that the ghost must have gone. Amanda made her way up the steps, then stood there for a moment as if in a trance, looking off toward the woods. Still half stunned at having her deepest guilt laid bare by a stranger who had felt no compassion but only a desire to make her suffer, she was hardly aware of her surroundings.

A cold gust of wind caused her to shiver in the darkness. Amanda stirred and looked around, suddenly aware of her situation. Marcie? What had happened to her? *Here I am worrying about myself and Marcie could be hurt,* Amanda thought. She ran around to the front of the house and rushed down the hall to the kitchen shouting Marcie's name. There was no reply.

Amanda used her flashlight to examine the hall and the kitchen, searching for any signs of Marcie, but everything seemed to be the way it had been when they had first entered. Amanda was about to head upstairs to look further when she spotted a key in the lock of the pantry door. She turned the key and pulled the door open.

Something rushed out at her, pushing her back against the counter.

"Stop!" Amanda shouted as hands reached for her throat.

"Is that you?" Marcie said, stepping back. "My God, is that really you?"

Before Amanda could respond, Marcie collapsed against her. Amanda had to put her arm around her to hold her upright.

"Get me out of here," Marcie murmured.

"You've got it," Amanda said, helping her to the door. "Just stay on your feet, and we'll be home soon."

Chapter Eleven

Marcie was lying on the bed and Amanda occupied the only chair. Both had cups of tea clutched in their hands and were looking at different points in the room as if afraid to meet each other's eyes. Marcie had hardly spoken in the car on the way back except to say in reply to Amanda's query that she wasn't hurt except for a few minor bruises. Already upset by her meeting with the ghost, Marcie's silence unnerved Amanda more than expressions of pain would have done. When they got back to the inn, Amanda had asked whether she would like a cup of tea and had gotten a nod in response. She had gone down to the kitchen and, not seeing Pat or her husband around, Amanda had searched around for the necessary items and made the tea for both of them.

Her tea almost gone, Amanda decided that it was time to talk.

"Do you want to tell me what happened?" she asked gently, looking directly at Marcie.

Marcie nodded but still didn't meet her glance.

119

"I stood in the doorway watching as you started down the stairs. All of a sudden a hand came around my mouth and someone pulled me backward out into the kitchen. I tried to get away, but he was strong."

"It was a man?"

Marcie thought for a moment. "I'm not sure. But it was somebody a lot bigger and stronger than me. Before I could even get my balance, he threw me into that closet and locked the door."

Amanda paused for a moment, not sure exactly how to phrase the next question. "I just happened to open the door to the pantry and find you. I could easily have missed seeing the key in the lock. Did you try banging on the door?"

Marcie drew her legs up and hugged them to her. She shook her head.

Seeing her usually strong friend looking almost child-like disturbed Amanda.

"Why not?" she asked softly.

Marcie gave a deep sigh, her breath coming out in ragged gasps as if she were about to cry.

"My dad used to lock me in the closet whenever I did anything wrong. He called it being thrown in the stock-ade. The more I shouted and banged on the door, the longer my sentence was." She looked up at Amanda and gave her a faint smile. "I guess I got used to being a good prisoner."

Amanda wanted to go over and give Marcie a comfort-ing hug, but she sensed that what she needed now was strength more than sympathy.

"Well, this guy, whoever he was, isn't your father. And we are going to teach him that he's just messed with the wrong two women. Do you understand me?"

Marcie nodded a little doubtfully.

"We aren't going to be good prisoners or frightened girls who go running back home at the first threat of danger," Amanda went on, aware that she was giving herself a pep talk as much as Marcie. "We are going to get to the bottom of what happened to Hazel Wilmot and what happened to you. Right?"

Marcie smiled weakly. "Yeah, that's right."

"Good," Amanda said, smiling back.

"What happened to you after I got mugged?"

Amanda paused, not sure how much of her experience she wanted to share with Marcie. Normally it would have been easy. She would have told an abbreviated version of the story, editing out any reference to her father and his death. But now that Marcie had confided in her, she felt an obligation to reciprocate and share some of the pain from her own past. Gradually, sticking with an objective, reporterlike tone, Amanda described what had happened. When she was done, it was clear that Marcie had forgotten her own bad experience and was completely caught up in Amanda's tale.

"How could she have known how your father died unless she was a real ghost?" Marcie asked.

"I've been sitting here for the last half-hour wondering the same thing myself," Amanda admitted. "When that woman was speaking to me in the basement, from behind the curtain and with that weird light, I'll admit that for a few minutes I thought that I was seeing my first real ghost. But I believe that I was just taken in by the atmosphere. Now that I've had a chance to calm down, I'm starting to realize that anyone who did a little research could have discovered how my father died. It was in the Boston papers. One of the reports, going for a human interest slant, even mentioned that he had been sitting up waiting for me to return home when the fire started."

"So this ghost woman could have guessed that you would feel guilty about your father's death?" Marcie asked gently.

Amanda shrugged. "Is it really so far-fetched? Wouldn't anyone feel a little guilty about something like that?"

"But you said that you got delayed on a story you were writing, and it certainly wasn't your fault that your father fell asleep with a burning cigarette in his hand."

"I knew he did that. His favorite chair had several burn holes in it. He used to joke about how he'd set himself on fire someday."

"And I'm sure you warned him not to do it."

"Of course."

"And he did it anyway."

Amanda nodded.

"So how is it your fault?"

"It's my fault because I told him that I'd be there to see him by nine, then I got held up on this story and forgot to call him. Maybe if I'd taken the time to give him a call, he wouldn't have fallen asleep. Then when I got there at ten-thirty he might have still been . . ."

Amanda stopped. The choking in her throat kept her from going on, and her chest began to heave in great, racking sobs. Marcie jumped off the bed and put her arms around Amanda as she began to cry.

"I'm sorry, I'm sorry," Amanda said a few minutes later when the crying had subsided. "I shouldn't be putting all this on you."

"Not a problem," Marcie said briskly, sitting on the end

of the bed and looking straight at Amanda, "as long as you're ready to stop being a good prisoner, too."

"What do you mean?"

"My father was a real louse who locked me up, but your father sounds like a nice guy who was a little careless. You're the one who's decided to punish herself for what happened even though nobody would ever say that it was your fault. Nobody has ever blamed you, have they?"

Amanda shook her head. "My mother and my brothers both told me not to beat up on myself. They said that the way Dad handled cigarettes, it was only a matter of time before a tragedy like that happened."

"But you wouldn't believe them. You figured that you were supposed to be perfect, so if something like that happened, somehow it must have been your fault."

"Maybe I am a little compulsive sometimes," Amanda admitted with a wan smile.

"That's what makes you a good editor, but maybe you should save that criticism for work and not be leveling it at yourself on your off-hours."

Amanda nodded thoughtfully.

Marcie stood up and glanced at her watch. "Midnight," she declared. "Do you think we should go back to the Shadsborough Inn and see what ghosts and goblins show up at the witching hour?"

"I think I'll give that a pass for tonight."

"Fantastic! One run-in with the supernatural in a night is enough for this girl. I guess I'll be off to bed."

"Thanks for the good advice," Amanda said.

"Yours wasn't bad either," said Marcie, giving Amanda's shoulder a squeeze as she headed for the door.

After Marcie left the room, Amanda sat where she was,

going over their conversation in her mind. There was an element of truth to what Marcie had said. Amanda knew that she had punished herself for her father's death, blaming herself far more than any minor oversight in not calling him that night deserved. Although she hadn't mentioned it to Marcie, she also knew why.

Her mother and father had divorced when she was twelve, largely because her mother had gotten tired of trying to deal with her father's alcoholism. Her mother had gotten custody of Amanda and her two brothers. The two boys, who were four and five years older than Amanda, had blamed their father for the breakup of their family and pretty much washed their hands of him. But although Amanda knew that her father could be silly and irresponsible at times, he was the one who fussed over her, told her stories, and bought her little gifts when he went on sales trips. She had continued to see him and had forgiven him.

But on that night when he had needed her most, she had let him down. And now she couldn't forgive herself. The only thing that made her feel a little better was visiting her mother frequently, as if one parent could be substituted for the other and the failure to save her father could be wiped away by looking after a mother who neither needed nor wanted such solicitous care.

Amanda sighed. She took off her clothes and put on her nightgown and robe. Although she didn't feel like it, Amanda knew that she should wash her face and brush her teeth before going to bed. When she reached the door, she heard Marcie humming softly to herself out in the hall as she returned from the bathroom.

A few words of truth and reassurance from me, and she

gets over her demons, Amanda thought enviously. *But no matter how much I talk sense to myself I still end up back where I started: standing on that street in Boston three years ago with the smell of smoke in the air.*

Chapter Twelve

When Amanda awoke the next morning, the sun was already high enough in the sky to cast a glow across her westward-facing room. Realizing in an instant that she had forgotten to set the alarm, she twisted around to look at the clock and saw that it was almost eight. She swung her legs out of bed and sat there for a moment, surprised to see Lost Trail Mountain framed in her window and looking quite cheerful with the morning sun reflecting off of it. *We shouldn't project human feelings on nature*, Amanda thought with a smile. *Nature just is. It's not good or bad. That only applies to people.*

Sensing that this line of thought would only bring her back to thinking about her father, Amanda jumped out of bed and headed down the hall to the bathroom. A few small puddles of water in the tub indicated that Marcie had already passed through, so Amanda got ready quickly. She entered the dining room just as the grandfather clock in the hall was striking 8:30. Marcie was sitting at the same table as yesterday with a glass of orange juice and a newspaper in front of her.

"Good morning, Sleepyhead," Marcie said, grinning.

"You're certainly an early riser."

"When you grow up in a military family it becomes ingrained," Marcie said. Then she frowned as if recalling the other behaviors that also became second nature. "I waited to order until you came down. I supposed you should pop into the kitchen and let Pat know that you're here."

Amanda nodded and walked out into the kitchen. Pat and her husband were sitting by the counter talking in low but urgent tones. Amanda cleared her throat to let them know she was there.

"Good morning," Amanda said, when Pat turned around.

"We've just had some very disturbing news," the woman said. "Stan was down at the police station this morning, and he heard that a hunter has found Anne Martin's body."

"This morning right around dawn," Stan added, as if further detail would somehow lessen the impact of the news.

"How did she die?" Amanda asked.

"They won't know for sure until the forensics team comes up from Concord, but the chief said it looked like she'd been hit on the back of the head."

"Was she found near the Shadsborough Inn?" asked Amanda.

"Nope," said Stan, rolling up the sleeves of his flannel shirt. "She was found on the other side of town. But the police aren't sure whether she died there or whether the killer moved her body. Judging by its condition, the body had been there for several days."

Pat Bennett's face tightened, and Stan reached over and took her hand.

"Under the circumstances, maybe Marcie and I should go somewhere else for breakfast this morning," Amanda suggested.

"No," Pat said firmly, getting up from the counter. "I'll be better off if I stay busy. It will help to take my mind off of things. I'll be right out with some coffee and to take your order."

Amanda nodded and returned to the dining room, where she told Marcie what had happened. Before they could say anything more, Pat came out and took their order. When she returned to the kitchen, Marcie leaned across the table.

"This is getting serious," she said in a low voice. "Are you sure that we shouldn't bail and leave this to the police? Now that the state police are involved, there's a better chance that the case will be solved."

Amanda bit her lip. "I'd be more convinced of that if I thought that Chief Hudson would emphasize to the state guys that there is a possible connection between Anne and what those boys saw in the inn. If he keeps quiet about that, the state police are never going to draw any connection between Professor Wilmot's death and Anne's."

"Well, we can't get involved in a state police investigation."

"We won't. We're going to concentrate on what happened to the professor. But I think if we can figure out what happened to her, there's a good chance we'll solve the mystery of Anne's death as well."

"Okay," Marcie agreed, but her expression remained uncertain. "What should we do next?"

"Give me a few minutes to think."

Pat came with their order. Marcie turned her attention to her breakfast, while Amanda ate slowly, staring off into space. When she'd finished her last swallow of coffee, Amanda carefully folded her napkin. Marcie hurriedly wiped up the last of the maple syrup with her remaining piece of waffle and glanced up expectantly.

"I think we have to find out two things. What actually happened that night when the boys went into the inn, and why Professor Wilmot told Middie Ross that there was a financial motive behind the appearance of the ghost."

Marcie nodded.

"I'm going to call Jimmy Racine's father and see if I can get to talk to the boy about what really went on that night. So far all we have is hearsay."

"Do you think he'll let you talk to his son? Parents can be pretty protective of their kids."

"He wrote a story about it in the newspaper, so he's hardly trying to conceal it. I'll tell him that I work for *Roaming New England* and want to do a follow-up article on what happened. That isn't far from the truth."

"And I have a bad feeling that you'd like me to make a return visit to Middie Ross."

Amanda nodded. "I'd like you to ask her if she has any idea why Hazel was so angry about the appearance of the ghost in the inn, and why she thought it had something to do with money. Maybe she'll think of something else if you ask her again. My experience has been that people usually know more than they tell you the first time."

"You're the expert," Marcie said, standing. "So it's

back to the witch's cottage for me. You realize that you owe me big time if I end up baked into a gingerbread cookie."

Amanda thought that she saw a look of genuine anxiety pass over of her friend's face.

"Are you all right with this? After last night, I mean."

"Get back on the horse once it's thrown you, that's one of the good lessons I learned from my dad." She paused for a moment as if thinking about him. "I'll be fine. You be careful too."

"I will," Amanda replied.

Middie Ross glanced up at the sound of the bell over the door ringing. When she saw that it was Marcie walking up to the counter, her eyes narrowed.

"Are you here to blame me for Anne Martin's death?"

"I didn't come here to blame you for anything," Marcie said. She did a little Irish jig in front of the counter. "I just wanted to show you how much the Saint-John's-wort helped."

"In one day it couldn't have helped you at all," Middie sniffed, but a small smile passed over her face at the sight of Marcie dancing. "You probably just recovered naturally."

"Well, I wanted to thank you anyway."

Middie nodded, then her eyes narrowed suspiciously. "But I'll bet you're here to ask me questions."

Marcie glanced around the store and saw that no one else was there, so it was safe to ask her questions. "Actually, I did want to ask you a little more about what you and Professor Wilmot talked about the last time you saw her," she admitted.

"I've already told you everything that I can remember,"

the woman replied. "Hazel thought there might be a connection between the happening at the Shadsborough Inn and the disappearance of Anne Martin. But I have no idea why she thought that to be the case. She got angry with me for suggesting that the ghost at the inn could have been a genuine supernatural phenomenon and stormed out without giving any reason for believing that."

"Did you talk about anything else?"

Middie frowned and her deep-blue eyes stared off across the store.

"Actually, we did. I'd forgotten because our last words were so harsh. She started off by asking me whether I had heard about any real estate schemes in town that Randy Markham might be involved in."

"I know that I've heard that name before," Marcie said slowly, trying to dredge it up from her memory.

"Markham has his main office in Concord, but he maintains a small branch here since he moved to town."

"Wasn't he the agent who got Professor Wilmot her house and the inn for Pat Bennett?" Marcie said, finally recalling the conversation Amanda and she had had the night before last in the kitchen.

"I believe that's true. Of course, he's really the only realtor in town. Mrs. Quimby used to be in the business, but she's pretty much retired now."

"Why did Professor Wilmot ask you about him?"

"Hazel said that she had just seen him the day before in a restaurant when she was having lunch down in Concord."

"And why did she think that he was involved in a real estate scheme here in Shadsborough?"

The woman shook her head. "I told Hazel that I hadn't heard anything about any real estate project being planned, and I asked her why she thought that Markham might be hatching something like that. She just said something vague about Markham having strange dining companions, then she changed the subject to the ghost in the inn and we got into an argument."

"The only real estate deal I've heard about is the plan John Phelps had to sell his land to a couple in Concord that wanted to fix up the inn," Marcie said. "Was Markham handling that deal for Phelps? Professor Wilmot could have been referring to that."

Middie smiled. "The last person John would have used as a go-between was Randy Markham. Markham tried to buy the land from John a couple of years back. He planned to sell it to a developer who was interested in putting up a senior citizens' community on the property. Of course, once John heard that the inn would be torn down, he wanted nothing to do with Randy's plan. I heard that Markham was rather persistent, and John's son threw him off the property."

The bell over the door rang again. Marcie turned and saw a woman of around her own age enter. She was slim, with her hair halfway down her back.

"Are we having our meeting tonight? There's a full moon?" the woman asked Middie.

Middie didn't answer but glanced at Marcie as if to say that she wanted to talk to her friend in private. Marcie took the hint, thanked the woman for her help, and left.

Amanda pulled up in front of the white colonial-style house. Overgrown bushes half-covered the front windows, and the white paint had peeled away in spots, giving the house a shabby look. Amanda had looked up Racine in the phone book. There was only one name list-ed, David Racine, which suggested that they weren't a long-established Shadsborough family. On the chance that someone would be home, she had called around nine o'clock and was surprised to find that he was still at home.

"I had to cover a water board meeting in Plymouth last night, so I get to work from home this morning," he explained when she identified herself and expressed pleasure in finding him at home.

"Well, I was wondering if there was a time today when I could talk with your son, Jimmy. I'm thinking about writing a piece for *Roaming New England* on the Shadsborough Inn."

"I see."

Amanda could sense the reluctance in his voice so she continued. "I know that you've already written about it in your newspaper, and I would certainly give you credit in my article."

"Hmm. But you see I was thinking about possibly turning it into a magazine article myself."

Amanda took a deep breath. Since she doubted that an article about this whole experience would ever appear in *Roaming New England,* she could promise David Racine almost anything.

"Perhaps, after I've written a short piece, if it provokes reader interest, we would be willing to publish a longer article written by you."

"Do you think so?" he asked happily, all pretense of being the tough negotiator disappearing.

"It's possible."

"Well, Jimmy happens to be home today. He has a little cold, so his mother thought he should stay in bed and get some rest. That's another reason why I'm here. She's a lawyer down in Concord and had to go in today. I figured I'd take Jimmy down to the paper with me for a couple of hours this afternoon."

Amanda wondered exactly how important David Racine's role was on the newspaper if he could work such a limited schedule. Maybe that explained why he was so anxious to exploit his son's story.

"Would it be possible for me to stop by this morning, then to have a talk with him?" she asked.

The man had agreed, and they set ten o'clock as the time to meet.

Now as Amanda walked up to the front stairs of the tired house, she hoped that Racine would prove to be as eager to snatch his moment of fame as he had sounded over the phone. Before she ever got to ring the bell, the door opened and a short, thin man of about thirty-five with dark hair, thinning in the front, quickly reached out a hand to greet her.

"Amanda Vickers, I presume," he said with a nervous laugh.

"Mr. Racine." Amanda shook his hand and stepped into the living room, barely avoiding the hand that he tried to place on her back to assist her.

"Jimmy is sitting in the kitchen having breakfast. Poor kid didn't feel like eating earlier."

Amanda followed the man to the back of the house. Sitting at the dining room table that barely fit in the kitchen was a boy of around ten. His nose was red, and he looked thoroughly miserable. Amanda said hello and forced herself to put out her hand. The boy touched it lightly, then returned to the toast on the plate in front of him. He carefully picked up the piece of bread and studied it like a sculptor contemplating a block of marble, then carefully took a bite from one end. To Amanda's eyes it appeared to have been nibbled in odd spots, forming some mysterious shape that was meaningful only to the boy.

"I'd like to ask you some questions about what you saw at the Shadsborough Inn. Is that okay?"

"We've already discussed it, and Jimmy has agreed to talk to you," his father answered quickly, causing Amanda to wonder how much pressure had been put on the boy to cooperate.

She studied Jimmy, trying to figure out how much he really wanted to talk to her. Reluctant interviewees were usually less reliable when it came to telling everything they knew. Of course, by the same token, overly willing ones were inclined to embellish the truth, which could be just as misleading. She guessed that Jimmy fell into the former category. Amanda took out her notebook and placed it on the table in front of her. She quickly skimmed the list of questions she had prepared. Whenever she interviewed children or the very elderly she liked to ask specific questions arranged in a sequence, because both groups often needed more guidance to stay on the point.

"Why did you go into the Shadsborough Inn that night in the first place?" she asked.

Jimmy gave the question a long moment's consideration as if weighing all the implications of his answer.

"The door was open, you know. The boys didn't break in," David Racine interrupted.

"I didn't say they did," Amanda said gently.

The man frowned. "Well, the police did. John Phelps told them that the doors were locked, and there was no way the boys could have gotten in without forcing them."

"Was there any sign of any doors being forced?"

David Racine shook his head. "That was the only thing that got the police off the boys' necks."

"The front door was unlocked," Jimmy said matter-of-factly.

"But why did you decide to go inside at all?" Amanda asked, returning to her list of questions.

"We saw lights."

"Where?"

"On the second floor."

"You've walked by the inn quite a lot at night, haven't you?"

"Oh, yeah. A group of us go out to Jason's every Monday night for our Cub Scout meeting, and we always walk back that way."

"Have you ever seen any lights in the inn before?"

He shook his head, then returned to nibbling on his toast.

"But you had already heard stories about the house being haunted?"

The boy paused, looking worried.

"No."

"But Miss Marston told me that only a couple of days before you saw the ghost, you mentioned that the inn was haunted. It was right after she read you that story about the headless horseman."

The boy smiled at the mention of the story. "That was a cool story."

"Like most boys his age, Jimmy is into that kind of thing," his father explained with an apologetic smile. "You know how kids are. A dark, deserted old house that's kind of spooky—they probably made up a story about the place, and Jimmy just repeated it in class."

"But Jimmy said in class that someone had told him that story."

The man gave a shrug as if to say that kids don't always tell the truth.

"Have you ever heard any legend about the inn being haunted?" Amanda asked the father.

He paused. "No, I guess not. But we've only lived in town for a couple of years. You'd be better off asking some of the old timers about that."

"Did an older person tell you about a ghost in the inn?" she asked Jimmy.

The boy shook his head. She heard David Racine clear his throat impatiently, so Amanda decided that it was time to move on.

"Okay. Now why don't you tell me about what you saw when you went inside?"

The boy went on to give an account that pretty closely matched what Amanda had already heard from Pat Bennett. Three of the boys had gone into the house and down the hall to the kitchen. The door to the cellar was open and a light was shining from down below. Only Jimmy went down the stairs.

"What did you see when you went down in the basement?" Amanda asked.

"I saw a girl wearing a white dress."

"A girl your own age."

"Older."

"As old as me?"

"You're not a girl," the boy said with certainty.

Amanda suppressed a smile. "Did you recognize her?"

"I couldn't see her face. It was too dark, and the light was sort of behind her."

"Did she say or do anything?"

The boy nodded solemnly and held his hands out in front of him with the palms up.

"She did that."

"And did she say anything?"

He nodded again.

"She said, 'Help me. Help me.' "

"And what did you do?" Amanda asked softly.

Jimmy bit his lip and looked down. "I ran away. I ran back up the stairs." He looked up at Amanda and she could see tears forming in his eyes. "I got scared and I ran away."

Chapter Thirteen

"I felt like a child abuser," Amanda said, shaking her head sadly. "You'd think that after all these years I'd have become toughened to conducting interviews. When I was on the paper, I talked to the next-of-kin of folks who had just been murdered or died in accidents, to people standing on the street outside their burning homes, to people who were the victims of all sorts of horrible things. I'd have to stand there and ask them how they felt."

"You ever get used to it?" Marcie asked.

"Not completely. Oh, you can pretty much guess what they're going to say. Still, it gets to you when you stand right there and hear them say it. But Jimmy Racine really surprised me when he admitted that he felt guilty about leaving the crying girl in the basement."

They were sitting in Amanda's room. Marcie was lying on the bed, and Amanda occupied the only chair. She had her spiral notebook open on her lap.

"Whoever set up that little scene at the inn was pretty

cruel," Marcie said. "They were really playing with those kids' emotions."

Amanda nodded. "And the more I hear about it, the more I think that it was carefully staged for that purpose."

"You mean whoever set it up knew when their scout meeting was going to be and when they'd be walking home?"

"Yeah. But that doesn't help to narrow down our list of suspects because probably half the people in town had that information." Amanda looked down at her notebook. "Another thing that bothers me is that Jimmy seemed very certain that he saw a girl in the basement, and by *girl* he clearly meant someone quite young."

"Anne Martin."

"Possibly. She had done some acting, after all. But then the question is, who did I see last night? Anne was already dead by then. The person I saw last night seemed older to me than a high-school girl, and I doubt that she would have fit Jimmy's definition of a girl."

"Okay, let's say it went this way: Somebody sets up this little play with Anne in the starring role. After the boys ran away, Anne and whoever was in charge of the scheme got into some kind of a dispute and Anne was killed. So last night another woman—someone older—had to fill in as the crying girl. How does that sound?"

"It fits the facts, but it doesn't get us any closer to knowing why the whole production was put on in the first place."

"Maybe I can help out there," Marcie said, and she went on to relate what Middie had told her about Randy Markham's desire to own John Phelps's land.

"Sounds like he might have had a good reason to spread negative publicity about the inn," Amanda said.

"Those folks down in Concord who were thinking about spending a small fortune to fix the place up and reopen it as an inn might change their minds if it turns out that the place is haunted."

"Wouldn't that actually help business by giving the inn a special appeal to people interested in the supernatural?" asked Marcie.

"If it were some charming old legend about a crime that happened long ago and vague stories about shadowy figures walking around the halls at midnight, it might not be a problem. But this was very recent, and it was a crying girl, not a nice quiet ghost. The overall effect is kind of menacing. People come out to a place like Shadsborough to get away from the dangers of the city for a few days. They aren't looking to tangle with something even worse."

"So Markham is definitely a suspect."

"The trouble is, I'm not sure that I can see how he would entice Anne Martin to get involved. We'll have to find out if there was any connection between them. Remember, Markham isn't the only one who would benefit from not having the Shadsborough Inn reopen."

Marcie nodded toward the door. "You mean the Bennetts?"

"They wouldn't be thrilled to have a fancy inn open right down the street. It would probably take away what little business they have."

"And Pat Bennett told us that she knew Anne." Marcie thought for a moment then shook her head. "Somehow I just can't see Pat—or Stan either, for that matter—as people who would plan something like this. And I certainly don't think that they would have murdered Anne Martin. Stan spent days helping the state police look for her."

"That's a pretty good cover," Amanda said.

"I suppose. But Stan just doesn't come across as a guy who would murder a young girl."

Amanda shrugged. "We can't let our impressions get in the way of the evidence. The problem right now is that we don't have enough evidence."

"So what do we do next?" asked Marcie.

"Ask more questions. I think we should pay Randy Markham a visit. Maybe we can find out more about his interest in the inn, and I'd also like to know who Hazel Wilmot saw him having lunch with that day in Concord."

"Yeah, according to Middie Ross, it really got Professor Wilmot thinking."

"I'd also like to pay Susan Marston another visit. She may know more about what the professor was thinking than she realizes."

"Which one do I get?" asked Marcie.

"Neither one."

Marcie groaned. "You aren't sending me back to talk to Middie Ross again, are you?"

"No. This time I want you to visit Mrs. Quimby."

"The retired realtor. Why her?"

"Think about it. She probably knows more about potential real estate deals in town than anyone, with the possible exception of Markham. She's been his competitor for years, so she probably has an opinion on what he's like as a person and a businessman."

"And why would she be willing to talk with me?"

"Because you're going to call her and express an interest in interviewing her for a piece you're doing on changes in the use of land in small towns for *Roaming New England.*"

"I'm not going to lie to this woman," Marcie said firmly.

"I wouldn't expect you to."

"You mean we're really going to do a story on land use in small towns?"

"I mean *you* are."

Marcie looked startled. "I've never written anything for publication."

Amanda smiled. "Well, then it's time you got started. Greg and I have both written articles for the magazine when freelance submissions were thin. It's about time you got started. This will look great on your résumé."

"But you and Greg are journalists."

"Which means that we just put down the facts. You don't have to be another Faulkner to write about real estate."

"What about conducting the interviews? I can't be wandering all over the region asking people questions."

"Use the phone or e-mail. Select a few towns of a certain size in each state and get in touch with the real estate agencies. If they know that their businesses will be mentioned in an article, they'll fall all over themselves to cooperate."

"But I start today with Mrs. Quimby."

"Right."

Marcie smiled in admiration. "You know, you can be pretty clever at times. In fact, one might almost say devious."

Amanda smiled back. "I know."

"Have you heard anything from Arthur Wilmot since he left town?" Marcie asked as she rolled off the bed.

"He left a voice-mail message on my cell phone. He's

at the motel and will stay there for two days. After that he has to go home. He told me we should report our findings to him."

"Quite the little leader, isn't he? Especially when he can do it from a safe distance. Do you think he'll really be any use to us?"

Amanda shrugged. "Right now I'm not sure how much help we're going to need."

Marcie headed for the door. "Well I sure hope that we don't end up having to rely on Arthur."

Chapter Fourteen

Marcie parked the rental car at the curb in front of the house where Martha Quimby lived. Amanda had told Marcie to use the car, since Randy Markham's office was on the same block as the library, and she could easily walk to both from the Lost Trail Inn. Marcie had looked up Mrs. Quimby's number in the phone book and called her from the inn, using the cover story that she was writing an article on the real estate market in rural New England. Although Mrs. Quimby had pointed out that she was semiretired and wasn't sure whether she could contribute much, the woman had quickly agreed with only the slightest of encouragement. Marcie suspected that the prospect of company was too good to resist.

The white clapboard house had a wraparound porch and was situated on a spacious corner lot with a stately oak tree occupying the central location. Quintessential New England, Marcie thought, as she went up the walk. But she did notice that the house could use a repainting and the garden beds seemed a bit overgrown, giving it the look of a place that had been cared for more carefully in the past than in the present.

The woman who answered Marcie's knock was short, plump, and gray-haired, wearing a white blouse and black skirt. A pair of reading glasses hung around her neck, and her smile revealed a set of straight white teeth that Marcie suspected might not be her own.

"Please come in, my dear," Mrs. Quimby said with a welcoming smile when Marcie introduced herself. She indicated a room to the right of the main hall. "Why don't we sit in the parlor. It doesn't get much use these days, and I always think that every room in the house should be used, don't you?"

Marcie sat down on a cushioned chair that sank beneath her rather alarmingly.

"I always have some tea and a little snack at around ten o'clock. Would you care to join me?"

Always ready to eat, Marcie nodded eagerly. When the woman returned a few minutes later with a tray that held a teapot and a plate with an assortment of homemade cookies, Marcie quickly helped her to set things up on the coffee table between them. In a few minutes, both were sipping tea, and Marcie was happily munching on a raspberry-preserves–filled cookie.

"So you said that you work for *Roaming New England* magazine, and you are gathering information for an article you plan to write on the real estate market in rural New England," Mrs. Quimby said.

Marcie nodded as she chewed, debating with herself whether taking another cookie from the plate so soon would make her look too greedy. She decided that this grandmotherly-type woman would be happy to see her eat and reached toward the plate.

"I'm afraid that I don't quite believe you," Mrs. Quimby said.

Marcie's hand froze in midair. She looked up in surprise at the woman's face, which still appeared kindly; however, Marcie could see a certain shrewdness she hadn't noticed before in her eyes.

"Excuse me?" she said, not quite sure that she had heard the woman correctly.

Mrs. Quimby smiled. "Well you see, my dear, I just can't believe that you happened to come all the way to Shadsborough to get my views on real estate."

"We're planning to survey other places as well," Marcie added desperately.

"But why start here and with me? Surely, you must have some other reason for being in town."

Mrs. Quimby smiled pleasantly and settled back in her chair as if willing to wait all day for an explanation. Marcie paused, then made the decision to come clean with this woman who clearly was a lot smarter than she first appeared. She told her about Hazel Wilmot's call and their attempts to investigate what was going on at the Shadsborough Inn. Mrs. Quimby listened intently until the end of the story, then she nodded.

"I wondered about the manner of Hazel's death myself. I knew her a bit and liked her. She never struck me as someone who would fall down a flight of stairs. And I did wonder what she was doing wandering around the old inn. You think it has something to do with Randy Markham?"

Marcie shrugged. "Only because the professor saw him in Concord a couple of days before she went to the inn, and on Friday she asked Middie Ross whether he was involved in any real estate deals."

Mrs. Quimby nodded slowly, then took a deep breath. She sat back and folded her hands across her stomach. Marcie got the sense that she was in for a lengthy story.

"The real estate business in Shadsborough has always been rather slow. Even though I was the only licensed realtor in town for many years, it was never more than a part-time business for me. Something I did to earn a little extra money while I was raising my family."

Her glance drifted over to a table that held the pictures of two men and a woman. In the center was a larger photo of an older man who clearly must have been her husband.

"My children are all grown and live some distance away now. When my husband died four and a half years ago and I suddenly had more time on my hands, I thought about the possibility of expanding my business a bit by advertising more and perhaps reaching out to some of the nearby communities."

"Did you?"

She shook her head. "Randy came to town before I could. He was charming, attractive, and already known for running a highly successful agency down in Concord. He rented office space in the center of town and bought a house right off the green, although I've heard that he kept his place in Concord and rents it out. He immediately became active in local civic affairs and made a lot of contacts."

"By doing that he pretty much shut you out of the market?"

An emotion that Marcie couldn't quite decipher came into the woman's eyes.

"It was a bit more than that. He began to suggest—suggest, mind you, not outright say—that perhaps I was getting a bit senile, too old to be entrusted with the responsibility of selling a person's most valuable piece of property. I heard this from an old friend who heard it from her daughter—a daughter who, I might add, believed it to be true. That's one thing about Randy, he's very believable. So, to make a long story short, before long what little business I had dried up."

"I'm sorry," Marcie said.

Mrs. Quimby smiled. "Thank you, my dear. But perhaps it's just as well. I am getting a bit too old to be out there hustling against the likes of Randy."

"So you obviously don't like him much."

"I don't like him, but he's always fascinated me. He's such an interesting puzzle."

"In what way?"

"Well, I doubt that even Randy, with all his aggressive methods, has been able to generate much more business than I had. Even if you include all the neighboring areas, there are rarely more than ten properties on the market at one time, and many of them remain unsold for upward of a year. I doubt that it even pays for the office space he rents and the girl he pays to be there to answer the phone while he's down in Concord."

"What about getting some farmers to sell their land for developments?" asked Marcie.

"It just isn't happening yet. We're still a bit too far out to be attracting people who want to build summer homes or ski lodges. And the few people interested in selling off their land are so far off the main roads that no one would be willing to develop the area."

"But didn't he try to get John Phelps's land?"

Mrs. Quimby nodded. "Now that's a different kettle of fish. The Shadsborough Inn property extends back from the main road and is very close to town. It's the closest thing around here to an ideal piece of real estate. The story that got around is that a major Boston developer was interested in building a large retirement community, over three hundred units, on the property. And Randy was their front man. He was going to handle the purchase of the property and the sale of the finished units. The commission would be worth a lot."

"Wouldn't the town have objected to such a large development?"

"Some would have. But Randy was in pretty tight with the so-called town fathers. Plus it would have done wonders for the tax base. People are pretty poor around here, and all those well-to-do retirees would have ended up making a nice addition to the town's revenues."

"But John Phelps refused to sell."

She nodded. "Once his wife died, reopening the inn became his memorial to her. It was his passion."

"I heard Michael Phelps threw Randy off the property."

The woman chuckled. "Michael had to do that or else his father would have shot Randy. Randy was really applying the pressure, coming out to see John every day and having John's old friends in town lean on him about the tax benefits of an expanding community. I'm sure Randy was furious when John dug in his heels and wouldn't budge. Randy must have felt that this was his chance to make a lot of money and here was a senile old man standing in his way."

Mrs. Quimby said the word *senile* with a special delight.

"So why didn't Randy close up shop and leave town when John Phelps refused to sell. Why keep an office open if he was probably barely breaking even?"

"I wondered about that for a while myself, then it came to me. Randy was planning to wait John out."

"But Randy couldn't have known that Phelps was going to get cancer."

"No, but John has been sickly for quite a while. I think Randy figured that it was only a matter of time."

"Who will inherit when John Phelps dies?"

"I imagine it will be his stepson, Michael."

"Michael wouldn't sell to Randy, would he? After all, he's the one who threw Randy off the property."

Mrs. Quimby smiled at the young woman's innocence. "What choice would he have? He's been trying to run the family roofing business with a few part-time helpers, but that's hard work and doesn't bring in a lot. There's probably not a lot left at the end of the year once he gets done paying taxes on all that property. Plus, what he'd get for that land would give him a tidy nest egg to start over somewhere else."

"But the land has been in his family for years."

"Not his family. Remember, he's John's stepson. Marsha was already a widow when she married John." Mrs. Quimby sighed. "I've known Michael since he and his mother moved to town when he was in his late teens. He's always been a nice boy but way too devoted to his mother. Marsha was a strong woman. She pretty much ran Michael and John. I don't think either one of them has been quite sure what to do with himself since her death."

"Randy was just hanging around then, waiting for John Phelps to die so he could buy the land?"

"Then John outsmarted him and found a buyer who wanted to restore the inn."

"Is that really true? Some people seem to think that's just a story John made up or a figment of his imagination."

"It was a solid deal. That couple in Concord were willing to make a fair offer on the land. Not what a big developer would bring to the table, but enough. More important to John, they were really going to fix up and reopen the inn."

"How do you know all this?"

Mrs. Quimby gave her a small smile. "I set it up."

Marcie sat there stunned for a moment then she laughed out loud.

"A little bit of revenge?"

"Well, no one likes to be called senile, my dear. I just wanted to show Randy that perhaps he had underestimated me." She paused for a moment, then frowned. "Unfortunately, all this ghost business has given the buyers cold feet. They've begun to doubt the likelihood of making a success of the inn now that it's gotten such an unsavory reputation. I've tried to convince them that the publicity will blow over, but they're unconvinced. They decided to back out of the deal. When I broke the news to John, he actually cried."

"This ghost thing has really played into Randy's hands," Marcie said. "Do you think that he could be behind it?"

Mrs. Quimby refolded her hands over her stomach and nodded. "I certainly wouldn't put it past him. He knew the people who were thinking about buying the inn, so he would have been aware that they are rather conservative folks who wouldn't want to own a property that was known for being haunted. But Randy couldn't have been directly involved in what happened that night."

"Why not?"

"On the night when Jimmy Racine saw the ghost, Randy was sitting right across from me at the local chamber of commerce meeting. It was our monthly dinner meeting, so it ran from seven-thirty to after ten. I believe that covers the time that the boys were seeing ghosts in the old inn."

Marcie nodded. "Of course, he could have hired someone to put on the performance."

"A possibility."

"Do you know of anyone he'd be likely to hire to do that kind of thing?"

Mrs. Quimby shook her head. "Nobody local. But Randy could have employed some people from out of town who might be willing to do that kind of thing, especially if they thought it was merely some sort of prank."

"Professor Wilmot's death was no prank," Marcie said.

"Of course, if you and your friend are right and the haunting is connected with Hazel's death, then that does change matters considerably."

Marcie nibbled on a cookie thoughtfully. "Even if Randy wasn't personally involved in the haunting, he could have been the one who murdered Professor Wilmot."

"Yes," the woman said slowly. "But although I'm reluctant to admit it, I find it rather difficult to picture Randy as a killer. A con artist, or possibly a thief, isn't much of a stretch, but I can't see him as a murderer."

"Possibly a double murderer," Marcie added, then went on to explain Amanda's view that Anne Martin may have been killed by the same person.

"Poor Anne, a talented young girl, but like so many young people, her high spirits were not tempered by good sense."

"Did you know her well?"

"I would run into her occasionally in the library. She worked there after school a few days a week. I had hoped that Susan Marston, the librarian, would be a calming influence on her."

"So there's no one in town that you think might be capable of these murders?" asked Marcie.

Mrs. Quimby's face saddened and she shook her head. "I was about to say that it must have been someone from outside because no one who lived here could possibly do such horrible things. But, of course, people in every town probably believe that, and killers, after all, have to live somewhere. But who really believes that their neighbors are capable of murdering innocent people? I'm afraid that we never know other people all that well, do we? At least not until it's too late."

The woman behind the desk at Markham's Realty was touching up her makeup when Amanda walked in the door. She took the time to carefully smooth some invisible lines away from her eyes and pat her hair before turning to smile politely at the potential customer. Amanda noted that the woman, who was approximately her own age, was very pretty and more stylishly dressed than anyone she had yet met in Shadsborough.

"Is Mr. Markham in?" Amanda asked.

"Oh, Randy's never here much after eleven in the morning. He spends most of the day down at the office in Concord. I'm Jennifer Ryan, may I help you?"

The way she said "Randy" with a special little inflection of warmth made Amanda wonder if Jennifer and Randy had something more than a purely business relationship. Amanda also wondered whether Jennifer could have been the woman who played the ghost last night at the inn. The age was right, and although she was seated, Amanda guessed that she was tall enough for the part.

"I just wanted to discuss the availability of real estate in the area with Mr. Markham," she said, hoping to get the woman to talk more to see if the voice was familiar.

The woman made a helpless gesture with her hands. "I'm not a realtor. I just answer the phone and make appointments for Randy, but if you could give me a more specific idea of what you're interested in then I can let him know when he comes in tomorrow."

"That's okay," Amanda replied with a smile. "I'll come back then and tell Mr. Markham myself. He will be in tomorrow morning, won't he?"

"I suppose. He usually is unless he calls," Jennifer said, looking worried in case Amanda were to return and not find Randy there.

"Don't worry. I'll give you a call first before I come back," Amanda assured her with a smile. "What time do you open?"

"Nine o'clock. Can I have your name, so I can tell Randy?"

"Amanda Vickers."

The woman jotted the name down on a pad next to her computer and gave Amanda a casual wave as she left the office. Amanda walked up the street toward the library, trying to decide if that could be the same voice she had heard in the basement last night. Although she tried to recall exactly how the ghost had sounded, last night's phantom had been angry and loud, while Jennifer had been so much more subdued that it made a comparison almost impossible. Amanda smiled to herself at the idea of going back and asking the young woman to shout "Get back murderer!" in order to make a more accurate judgment of her voice.

If Jennifer had played the ghost, she certainly was a cool customer because she had showed no sign of concern when I announced my name. Amanda thought. *Of course that doesn't mean much because whoever was playing the part had to be an actress and would be good at disguising her emotions.*

Susan Marston was down the center aisle shelving books when Amanda entered.

"Need some more help?" she asked with a smile.

Amanda sighed and nodded.

"Not getting anywhere with your investigation?"

"You could hardly call it an investigation," Amanda said, wanting to play down what she was doing. "I'm just asking people questions and not getting much in the way of answers. I was hoping that maybe you could remember a little more about what Professor Wilmot talked about the last time you saw her."

Susan furrowed her brow. "Like I said, she asked me about the story surrounding the Shadsborough Inn ghost, and I told her about the research that I had done."

"Did she say anything about Jimmy Racine?"

"She did ask me to repeat what went on in the class that day, and I told her pretty much what I told you."

"Did Jimmy ever say where he got the story from?"

Susan shook her head. "Just that someone had told him. Why?"

"That's what Jimmy told me, too, but the idea of there being a ghost in the inn doesn't seem to be exactly common knowledge. Pat Bennett wasn't aware of it, and Jimmy's father hadn't heard about it."

"Of course, they're both newcomers to town. Maybe

someone who had been in town longer told him about it. But Jimmy didn't repeat the story in all the detail that I gave you, so maybe he just made up a story about a spooky-looking house. Perhaps he didn't want to admit in class that he'd fabricated the whole thing, so he claimed that he'd heard it somewhere."

"And it happened to turn out to have a history behind it?"

Susan shrugged and smiled. "If you dig back far enough, lots of houses in any old New England town have strange stories associated with them."

Amanda shook her head. "I still think someone told him about the ghost in the inn. Did the materials you used for your research have any connection to a family still living in town."

"No, the items didn't have any labels or notes saying who originally gave them to the library."

"Too bad."

"Well, let me give this some thought," Susan suggested. "Maybe I can come up with the names of older persons who like to tell stories. I can ask around and find out if anyone told Jimmy about it."

Amanda thanked her and started for the door. "By the way, did Professor Wilmot ever say anything to you about her lunch in Concord that week?"

"No, I didn't even know she went down there. Was it significant in some way?"

"I'm not sure. All I know is that she saw Randy Markham having lunch at a restaurant down there."

Susan laughed. "That's not too surprising. Randy has a business down there, and he loves to socialize. He even manages to do some of it here in Shadsborough, which isn't easy."

"Do you know him well?"

"Hardly at all. A librarian isn't exactly one of the movers and shakers in town. He's more friendly with the members of the chamber of commerce."

Amanda nodded.

"What are you going to do next?" asked Susan.

"Maybe I'll try talking to Jimmy again to find out where he got his ghost story from."

"I'll keep working on it from my end," Susan promised.

"Why don't I give you my cell phone number?" said Amanda. She recited the numbers, and Susan wrote them down on a small slip of scrap paper that she took from a pile on the counter.

"Between us we should come up with something," Susan said.

"Let's hope it's soon," Amanda replied.

Chapter Fifteen

Amanda hurried across the gravel parking lot of the Lost Trail Inn clutching the collar of her light jacket to her throat, anxious to get inside. Although it was just going on 4:00, the sun was already disappearing behind the mountain and a chilly breeze swept across the front lawn of the inn.

As soon as she got into the lobby and took off her coat, Amanda saw an inviting fire blazing in the parlor fireplace. The warm, rosy glow drew her into the room where she saw Marcie sitting on the sofa, eating an apple and leafing through a magazine. As she walked closer, Amanda recognized a back issue of *Roaming New England* that had contained an article of her own.

"Always working," Amanda said, settling into a leather club chair across from the sofa.

Marcie grinned. "I figured that if I'm going to have to write one of these things, I'd better look back and see how you and Greg do it."

"You'd be better off studying one of Greg's. He's got more experience."

"I'm enjoying yours."

Amanda nodded and looked around the room with appreciation. "It's getting cold outside. Too bad we can't eat in here. The fire makes it nice and cozy."

"Does that mean we don't have to go chasing ghosts at the Shadsborough Inn tonight?" Marcie said with an evident note of relief in her voice.

"I guess not. I think the solution to these crimes is going to involve getting evidence from other places."

"What other places?"

Amanda held up a restraining hand. "Why don't we start by telling each other what we've learned this afternoon? You begin."

Between bites from her apple, Marcie reported on her visit with Mrs. Quimby. She somewhat guiltily admitted to telling the woman about their investigation.

"I didn't think she'd tell me anything otherwise. Was that the wrong thing to do?" she asked Amanda.

"What other option did you have? She's clearly a shrewd lady and guessed that you were up to something. Probably being open with Mrs. Quimby got her to be equally open in her responses. I know you may not think that I believe this, but sometimes honesty is the best policy."

Marcie nodded. She repeated Mrs. Quimby's story about Randy Markham's questionable business practices, and concluded with a summary of his connection to John Phelps and the old inn.

"So Mrs. Quimby thinks that Randy is just waiting for John Phelps to die so he can get his hands on the inn and the surrounding property?"

"Yep. She says that it will be a really great deal for

Randy if he can sell it to a big developer of senior housing once John Phelps is dead."

"And she thinks that Michael Phelps would be willing to do business with Randy?" Amanda asked.

"Doesn't think he has much choice, I imagine. According to Mrs. Quimby, he won't be able to afford to keep the land anyway."

"I wonder if Markham and Michael Phelps were the two people Professor Wilmot saw eating in Concord. That would probably get her thinking that the two of them had staged that little ghost show at the inn in order to scare off John Phelps's buyers."

"But why would Michael want to foul up his father's deal?" asked Marcie. "The money that his father would get from the couple in Concord would come to him eventually."

"Sure. But Michael will get a lot more from Markham's big developer."

Marcie stared at the fire thoughtfully for a few seconds. "Okay. But Markham couldn't have actually been there that night when Jimmy saw the ghost because Mrs. Quimby said he was at the chamber of commerce meeting."

"So Michael Phelps staged the whole thing by himself. That means he might also have been the one who killed Anne Martin," Amanda suggested. "And although I didn't get to see Randy Markham, I do have a possible candidate for last night's ghost." Amanda went on to tell Marcie about her conversation with Jennifer Ryan.

Marcie nodded. "So Michael and Randy are in on this scheme together. They used Anne Martin as their ghost, but then Michael kills her because she does something that makes him nervous. Maybe she had some doubts about what they were up to, or she threatened to tell some-one about their little show."

"So when they decide to put on a performance for me, they pull in Jennifer as a substitute because she'd do any-thing for Randy."

"Sounds good," Marcie said. "Plus if Michael Phelps was involved that would explain why the door to the inn was unlocked so the kids could get inside, and then was unlocked again on the night that Professor Wilmot died. Even if his father did secure the place, Michael Phelps would be able to get the keys."

"The problem is we can't prove any of it," Amanda said with a frown. "We can't actually place Michael Phelps or Anne at the inn that night. Nor do we have any proof that he was in the inn the night Professor Wilmot died. We have motive and opportunity, but no solid evidence to prove that our theory is true."

Marcie was about to speak, when Amanda's cell phone rang. She listened for a few seconds, then promised to be right over.

"Where are you going?" Marcie asked Amanda when she had disconnected.

"That was Susan Marston. She was looking over the materials on the ghost at the inn and spotted something she wants me to look at. She thinks that there may be a connection between the story and one of the more promi-nent families still in Shadsborough that could be worth checking out."

"Do you want me to come along?"

"Susan suggested that I bring you along, but I really don't see any point. When I come back, we can go out for something to eat and go over any new evidence that she has."

After Amanda left, Marcie continued leafing through the issue of *Roaming New England* but found herself getting restless. The warm, cozy room suddenly seemed stuffy, and she felt the need for some fresh air. After getting her fleece jacket from her room, Marcie stopped in the kitchen to tell Pat Bennett that she was going out for a walk.

When she reached the end of the driveway, she turned right, deciding to walk away from the center of town and Lost Trail Mountain. Twilight had begun to settle in deeply by now, and Marcie decided that she would only walk as far as Arthur Wilmot's house. She wanted to be back by the time Amanda returned because she was already getting hungry.

At first Marcie thought that Arthur's house was in complete darkness. But when she walked past the front and turned around, ready to return to the inn, she spotted a light on in a back corner room.

Maybe he left a light on a timer for security, Marcie thought. But she wondered whether someone who was going to be away for an indefinite amount of time would really do that, so she walked across the lawn and around the back of the house to check it out.

The window into the lit room was a little high for her to see into directly, but Marcie figured that if she went up on the porch and leaned over the railing she could just manage to peek into the room. Trying to walk softly up onto the wooden porch so as not to alert whoever was inside, Marcie leaned out over the rail and peered through the window that was covered by only a sheer curtain. The room, which turned out to be the kitchen, appeared to be empty, although a grocery bag was in the center of the table.

"What are you doing there?" a voice shouted behind her, causing Marcie to almost topple off the porch. She spun around ready to fight or run. There at the foot of the step stood Arthur Wilmot, staring up at her owlishly.

"Marcie?" he said.

She took a deep breath to slow down her breathing and get her voice under control.

"I thought you were going to stay out at that motel," she finally managed to gasp.

He shuffled his feet and studied his shoes. "Yeah. Well, there really wasn't much for me to do there, and I figured that I might as well get started packing up some of my mom's things. I'll have to do it eventually." He moved up the stairs toward her. "I guess I also got to thinking about what you said about my running away and decided that maybe I shouldn't let myself get scared off so easily."

"Good for you," Marcie said, hitting him lightly on the arm. "I wondered who was here when I saw the grocery bag on the kitchen table, but no one seemed to be around."

"Yeah, I'd just been out buying something for dinner. I guess I was behind the garage putting stuff in the garbage when you came up the driveway. Sorry if I startled you."

"No problem. I was just doing a little security check."

Arthur nodded and shuffled his feet some more. Feeling sorry for this nervous guy who was planning on eating his dinner alone, Marcie suggested that they go back to the inn and meet Amanda. The three of them could then go out to dinner together. Arthur quickly agreed, and they took his car for the three-block ride back to the inn. When they walked in the front door, Pat Bennett was there to greet them. She seemed surprised for a moment to see Marcie with a man, but once she recognized Arthur, she greeted him warmly.

"Susan Marston just called. She wanted me to tell you that she and Amanda are going out to the Shadsborough Inn to check out some new piece of information. Amanda wants you to meet them out there."

"There goes an early dinner," Marcie moaned. "Oh, well, I guess work comes first."

"Can I come along?" Arthur asked.

"Sure, this has as much to do with you as with us."

On the ride out to the inn, Marcie told Arthur about their most recent thinking on what had happened. She shared her frustration with their being unable to prove anything.

"It sounds like you've come up with a pretty good theory except for one thing."

"What's that?"

"Michael Phelps couldn't have had anything to do with the death of my mother because I met him at the airport when I flew in on the day after her death. We knew each other from around town. He told me he was coming back from a builder's convention down in Philadelphia. His father had insisted that he go to get some tips on drumming up business. I think Michael felt it was a waste of time."

"How long was he gone?"

"Three days."

"Are you sure he was really there?"

Arthur shrugged. "He was carrying a plastic bag with some kind of builder's logo on it."

Marcie sighed. "Well, I guess we'll have to modify our theory a little, but he still could have been involved in the original haunting episode."

"He certainly would benefit along with Markham if the inn property was sold to developers."

Arthur signaled, even though there were no other cars in sight, and they pulled off onto the gravel drive down toward the inn. Smiling to herself Marcie realized that this was the first time she'd been to the Shadsborough Inn when she had actually pulled into the driveway instead of concealing the car somewhere along the road. A compact car she assumed to belong to Susan Marston was parked by the front door. There were no lights on in the inn, but that was to be expected since there was no electric power. Marcie grabbed the flashlight she had taken from her room before they left.

They got out of the car and walked up to the front door.

"What's that you're carrying?" Marcie asked, as the beam of her flashlight washed over Arthur.

"A tire iron," he said, waving it in front of him.

"Do you really think you'll need that?" asked Marcie, rolling her eyes in the darkness.

"I haven't had a lot of good luck in this house. I'm coming prepared."

"Once again the inn is unlocked," said Marcie, as she turned the handle of the front door and it opened. "For a place that's supposed to be secure, this building is as open as the average bus terminal."

"You know, it occurs to me that all this is a little odd," Arthur said nervously. "I mean the door should be locked and boarded up."

"I guess. Maybe Susan and Amanda took off the boards."

"Would they have the key?"

"The only way to find out is to go inside and ask them," said Marcie, pushing the door open. She paused on the threshhold. "You know, Art, no one knows that you're in town, and Amanda always said that you were our backup. Maybe you should wait out here until I give the all-clear."

"You want me to wait out here?" He glanced around. "It's dark and it's cold."

"You can wait in the car."

"Okay," he said, pulling the key from his pocket. "But don't get all wrapped up in things and forget that I'm out there."

Marcie grinned and stepped into the hall. "Don't worry. I won't forget you."

She stood in the lobby for a moment trying to detect the sound of voices, but heard only the creaks of the old house. Guessing that if people were walking around upstairs she would hear them, Marcie walked toward the back of the house.

I should have known, Marcie thought, *that I'd end up in that basement again.*

Marcie kept checking behind her to be sure that she wasn't being followed, and she was especially careful to shine the flashlight over the door to the closet where she'd been imprisoned. She pushed open the door to the cellar. Just like last time, a light was burning somewhere in the cellar, casting a flickering glow over the downstairs, but this time the light was quite a bit brighter. Marcie still wasn't taking any chances.

"Hello," she called from the top of the stairs, "anyone down there?"

A tall young woman appeared at the bottom of the stairway.

"Hi, Marcie, we're down here," she said.

Marcie went down the stairs.

"Hi, I'm Susan Marston," the woman said, extending her hand. "Amanda's right over there."

Marcie saw Amanda in profile, leaning back against one of the support beams just outside the glow of a kerosene lantern.

"What's up, Amanda?" Marcie asked, walking over to her friend.

Amanda's face turned toward her, but she didn't say anything. Only when Marcie got closer did she see that a gag was tied over her mouth.

"What's going on here?" Marcie asked, running to pull the gag from Amanda's face. At the same time, she saw that Amanda's hands were tied behind her back and around the wooden beam.

"I'm sorry," Amanda said, once the gag was removed. "I couldn't warn you."

"You can untie her hands too, if you want," said Susan.

Marcie turned and saw that there was a gun in the woman's hand.

"I only tied and gagged her so she wouldn't be able to warn you before we had you both in the cellar."

"Who's 'we'?" Marcie asked, working at untying the knots in the rope that bound Amanda's hands.

A man walked into the light from the far end of the basement.

"Who's he?" asked Marcie.

"Michael Phelps," said Amanda softly. "At least we had part of it right."

Her hands now free, Amanda began massaging her wrists and stretching her arms to get back the circulation.

"Is everything set back there?" Susan asked sharply.

"Yes," the man said with an unhappy expression.

"Good. Go open the door, then take care of that floorboard upstairs."

The man walked past the women, not meeting their eyes. He went up a short series of stone steps behind them and opened the cellar door to the outside. A cool gust of air immediately rushed down into the basement. Amanda tried to suppress a shiver.

"Sorry that it's so chilly right now," said Susan, "but that won't last for long."

Michael Phelps walked back across the basement and up the inside stairs.

"Remember, be careful not to leave tool marks," Susan said to his back. "And don't bother coming back down here. Go around to the back and be ready when I come out."

The man mumbled an affirmative.

A few moments later, they heard some muffled hammering.

"Do you mind telling me what's going on here?" demanded Marcie.

"I'd be happy to. What we are doing is setting the scene for the final act of our play. Michael just finished poking some holes in that old oil tank back there before you arrived. Apparently it still had some fuel in it, and that is now seeping into those boxes of old linens and draperies. He brought along a bit more oil in case there wasn't enough in the tank, so everything will be well soaked when the lantern accidentally falls over and ignites them."

"And what's he doing now?" Marcie asked.

"Only guaranteeing that a floorboard will pop up just enough to make it impossible for the door from the cellar to the kitchen to open and allow the two of you to escape, should you be lucky enough to make your way through the smoke and up the stairs."

Marcie glanced over her shoulder to the stairs leading outside.

"That's the way I'll leave. Unfortunately, I'll have to chain and padlock the door for security as I go. So I'm afraid that you will have no means to escape."

"But why are you doing this?" Marcie asked, hearing her voice rising with panic.

"Because she killed Anne Martin and Hazel Wilmot," Amanda said.

Susan nodded her agreement. "True. But ultimately I'm doing it for the money. Michael and I are going to get married, and once he has the money from the sale of this land, I'll be able to get out of this God-forsaken place."

"You and Michael!" Marcie said.

"I know he isn't exactly the most exciting guy in the world, I admit, but he'll do anything I say. I have to give his mother credit. She certainly trained him well when it came to taking orders from the woman in his life."

"How long have you two been together?" asked Amanda.

"I've been seeing Michael in secret ever since I found out that his father was dying. I'd heard about Randy Markham wanting the land, and that made Michael an appealing prospect. We had to keep our relationship quiet. His father didn't exactly approve of me because I wasn't from around here. Turned out that in the long run it was just as well. That way, no one ever suspected my involvement in the haunting."

"Was there ever really a ghost in the Shadsborough Inn?" Amanda asked.

Susan nodded. "I couldn't believe my luck. I was desperate when I heard that John had found a couple who wanted to reopen the inn. I'd invested over a year of my life in Michael, and I didn't know what to do. Then I happened to be reading in the archives during one of the slow times at the library, and I found this book telling the story about the ghost in the inn. But I still had to figure a way of getting it out in public in a way that would make news without directing attention to myself."

"That's where Jimmy Racine came into the picture," said Amanda.

"Right. I told the story to Jimmy when he was in the library one day. We decided to play a little game with his class, where he'd tell them about the ghost on the day I read about the headless horseman. But he had to promise not to tell anyone where he got the story. I knew that once Jimmy and his friends heard about the ghost, they'd be keen to get inside the house. So I figured I'd put on a little show for them. I knew that Jimmy's dad would do anything for a feature that would get him some publicity, and he'd spread it all around the Concord area. You have to admit, it worked perfectly."

"So that's why I'm here," Amanda said suddenly. "When I told you that I planned to talk to Jimmy again, you got worried that he'd admit that he first heard the story from you. That would get people thinking that maybe you had staged the entire episode, using Anne Martin as the ghost."

"I thought that I could trust Jimmy to keep our little secret, but I couldn't be sure."

"Just like Anne Martin," Amanda pointed out.

"Too bad about Anne. We were like sisters working together in the library. She reminded me of myself when I was her age, ready to do just about anything to get ahead."

"But she had second thoughts?" asked Amanda.

"I told her we were just going to play a little prank on those kids. Anne was always anxious to show what a good actress she was, so she really threw herself into the part." Susan gave a short laugh. "I was hiding in the basement at the time, and she even had me believing she was a ghost. But when Anne saw how scared Jimmy was when he ran away, she said that we had to tell the boys that it was just a joke."

"But you couldn't have her doing that," Amanda said.

Susan shook her head. "We argued about it right over there." The woman pointed to the open stairwell leading to the outside. "She wanted to go right over to Jimmy's house and tell him the truth. I grabbed her arm to stop her, she shoved me, and I shoved her back. She fell and hit the back of her head on the edge of the concrete step."

"And you dumped her body in the woods," Marcie said, sounding more angry than afraid.

Susan heard the change of tone and raised her gun. "Don't get any ideas. I know how to use this." She smiled. "This is Hazel's gun. How's that for a nice touch of irony?"

"And why did you kill Hazel?" Amanda asked, giving Marcie a warning glance.

"After she saw Randy Markham and Michael having lunch together in Concord, she began to wonder about the ghost that the boys had seen. She thought that Randy and Michael had made it all up. She came to me and wanted to know if the story was true. I showed her the book and thought that would be the end of it. But the next day she came back and wanted to know how Jimmy had heard the story if I had only found out about it after hearing him talk about it in class. I said I didn't know, and she decided to go talk to Jimmy herself. I knew that she could browbeat the truth out of almost anyone, so I told her that maybe we should take a look at the basement ourselves. That way she could ask more detailed questions when she talked to the boy."

"That must have appealed to Professor Wilmot's scientific side," said Amanda.

Susan nodded. "I told her that I'd bring a crowbar so we'd be able to get inside somehow. Hazel's opinion of Chief Hudson was so low that she had no qualms about breaking the law."

"But you didn't meet her. How did you know she'd go in the house alone?"

"I'd taken the boards off and unlocked the front door. I knew that Hazel wouldn't pass up the chance to look around."

"And you were waiting in the basement to kill her."

"It had to be done. If it's any consolation to you, I never intended that anyone would get hurt. All this is just damage control."

"Your plan really depended a lot on Jimmy keeping the secret about where he heard that story," said Marcie.

Susan smiled and glanced upstairs to where they could hear Michael Phelps walking down the hall and out of the inn. "I've always had a way with boys."

"And you were the one who played the ghost for me the other night?"

The woman nodded. "I was afraid you might recognize me, so I had to be careful to stay behind the curtain, where you would only see me in silhouette. And I stayed seated, so you wouldn't be able to guess my height."

"How did you know about the way my father died?"

"I am a trained librarian, after all, and the Internet is a wonderful thing."

"And was it Michael who locked me in the closet?" asked Marcie.

Susan nodded. "The first time he's gotten his hands dirty," she said with contempt.

She waved the gun. "Now you two walk over there," she said, motioning them toward the end of the basement where the boxes were piled.

Amanda pretended to gag at the smell of the fuel oil and coughed.

"We have to do something," she whispered quickly to Marcie. "Maybe if we both rush her, one of us will get the gun away from her."

"Don't do anything foolish," Susan warned. "I'm a good shot. You wouldn't want to be wounded and lying helpless on the floor as the fire creeps up to you."

"You won't get away with this. Pat Bennett knows that you're here with us," Marcie said desperately.

"But what she doesn't know is that I left right after you arrived. I offered to take Amanda back to the library to pick up her car, but the two of you wanted to stay around to investigate a while longer. That's why I left the lamp. Although I did warn you to be careful with all the flammable things around here, I guess one of you got careless. And who knew about the leaking tank?"

She took a small flashlight out of her pocket, and with the same hand, she seized the lantern off the box it was setting on and casually tossed it in the direction of the oil-soaked rags. There was a sound of breaking glass, then a moment of silence.

Looking over Susan's shoulder, Amanda saw a figure

coming down the cellar stairs. She expected to see Michael Phelps and was surprised when it turned out to be the ungainly figure of Arthur Wilmot. With the exaggerated movements of a bad actor trying to portray stealth, he crept up behind Susan, the tire iron raised high in his hand, while Amanda and Marcie tried to look elsewhere so as not to give him away. When he was about ten feet away from Susan, his foot scraped loudly on the dirt floor.

For Amanda several things seemed to happen at once: Susan turned quickly, Marcie ran toward her, the gun went off, and with a tremendous "Wump!" a ball of flame exploded behind her, scorching the back of her neck. Marcie's charge had spun Susan around, but she still had the gun in her hand. As she raised it to fire at Marcie, who was struggling to regain her balance for a second attack, Amanda plowed into Susan and sent her sprawling, the gun skittering across the rough floor of the cellar. Instantly Susan was on her hands and knees crawling toward the gun, as Amanda jumped on her back.

Amanda was tightening her grip around Susan's waist to pull her away from the gun when a gray cloud suddenly filled the room. Amanda took a breath, and the hot acrid smoke filled her lungs, leaving her coughing and gasping. Susan slithered out from under her, disappearing into the bank of smoke. The only illumination came from the flames raging at the far end of the basement that were being fed by the still-open basement door.

Keeping her face close to the floor, where a blanket of cool air still seemed to be available, Amanda stopped coughing long enough to assess what she should do next. With all the smoke, there was little likelihood of Susan spotting her even if she got the gun. Her best bet was to head toward the fresh air and hope that would lead her out of the basement. If Susan was waiting for her there, she'd deal with that problem when she came to it. But where were Marcie and Arthur? She pushed the question away. There was nothing she could do to help them now. She could barely help herself. Maybe they would find their way to the stairs as well.

Remaining belly-down on the floor, Amanda turned until she felt the cool breeze on her face, then she began to slide forward along the rough floor, feeling the grit tear at her clothing. She had gone about four feet, hoping that her hands would soon feel the bottom step, when the breeze suddenly disappeared. Faint from the lack of oxygen, Amanda put her head down on the floor, feeling helpless. Someone had closed the cellar door! She was trapped. There was no point in trying anymore. She lay there thinking that this wasn't much different from going to sleep after a hard day.

A hand roughly shook her shoulder. She rolled over on her side and looked up. Through the thick smoke she saw her father's face looking down at her.

"Mandy, girl, what are you doing just lying there? You have to get going," he said with the same smile he gave her on those mornings when he'd wake her to go to school.

"I'm so tired, Daddy, can't I sleep a little while longer?"

"Not right now, sweetheart, we have important things to do."

"But it's so dark, I can't see anything. Where should I go?"

"Just come with me, Mandy," he said, reaching out his hand. "Everything will be fine."

Amanda felt the work-roughed skin of his hand in hers, and she began to crawl along beside him. Although she paused to cough several times, he insistently pulled her along whenever she tried to stop.

"Where are we going, Daddy? It's so far."

"It won't be long now, honey. Reach out with your left hand, do you feel that?"

Amanda's hand touched wood.

"That's the coal bin. We're going to go in the coal bin," he said encouragingly.

"Why?"

"You'll see. Keep crawling. It won't be long now."

Amanda's head bumped into something.

"We've reached the wall now, Mandy. You need to climb up on something. There! To your right. I think I see a wooden box. Climb up on that."

Staggering, Amanda slipped off the box a couple of times before managing to get her balance by leaning against the dirt wall.

"Good girl," her father said. Now reach right in front of you. Do you feel a metal handle?"

Amanda's hands searched along the wall until they finally found a piece of metal protruding from the wall.

"Pull on it, Mandy."

Amanda pulled with all her strength, but nothing happened. "It's stuck."

Her father's hand came on top of her own and squeezed. "You have to pull harder, honey."

She screamed as her father's hand crushed her own, and she pulled harder than she ever had in her life. With a sudden popping sound, the door flew inward, almost causing her to fall from the box. Cool air rushed over her and she took a deep breath.

"Good work, honey," she heard her father say in her ear. She turned around to look behind her and saw her father seeming to float right behind her. "Now crawl out through the opening."

"Come with me, Daddy!"

He gave her a gentle smile. "I can't, Mandy."

"But I'm sorry for what I did."

"You didn't do anything, honey. Whatever happened I did to myself. I never blamed you, so don't you go blaming yourself."

He reached out and put his arms around her, and Amanda felt a soothing warmth flow through her body.

"What you can do for me now is to go on living."

He lifted her up until her head and shoulders were in line with the opening. She clung to his neck until he gently but firmly took her arm away.

"Good-bye, Daddy," she cried.

With a sudden shove, Amanda felt herself being forced through the narrow opening. For a moment she thought she would be stuck, then she pushed with her hands and suddenly popped out onto the ground.

She slowly got to her feet and began to stagger toward the flashing lights that seemed very far away. She continued walking, slipping to one knee, then getting up again and forcing herself to go on. It was like a dream where you keep walking and walking but never reach your destination. Just as she was about to fall, a pair of arms came around her waist, holding her up.

"It's okay now," she heard Marcie say.

Chapter Sixteen

Amanda lay on her bed back at the Lost Trail Inn. The EMTs had treated her at the scene for smoke inhalation, a few scrapes, and a minor burn on the back of her neck. They'd wanted to take her to the hospital, but Amanda had insisted that she felt fine. Finally the ambulance attendants had given up, admitting that she was in amazing shape for someone who had been down in that cellar for so long.

She looked over at Marcie, who seemed to be dozing in the chair next to the bed. Chief Hudson had wanted to take them down to the station for questioning, but Pat Bennett arrived at the scene of the fire and insisted that both of the young women needed to go to bed immediately. There would be time enough for questions in the morning. They had remained silent on the ride home. Marcie and Amanda were too tired to speak, and Pat was unwilling to disturb them.

Amanda reached over and took a sip from the mug of

mulled cider on the bed table beside her. Marcie opened her eyes.

"A tough night," she said.

Amanda nodded. "That's an understatement."

"Maybe we should talk about what happened before turning in," said Marcie. "I don't want to wake up in the middle of the night with a million questions. You left the inn and went to the library to see Susan. What happened next?"

"I guess I won the gullibility award. Susan said she had something to show me. The next thing I knew there was a gun pointing at me. She made me drive her car to the inn. That's where she met Michael Phelps and made the call to Pat Bennett. Susan wanted to kill both of us because she was afraid we'd eventually figure out that she was behind the ghost scam and the murder of Anne and Hazel. She didn't expect Arthur to tag along. By the way, how did Arthur end up back in town?"

Marcie explained about his change of heart.

"How did you and Arthur manage to get out of the cellar?" Amanda asked.

"Well, I saw you struggling with Susan. I was coming to help you when the smoke rolled in. I tried to find you, but I got completely turned around. I was searching for you when I tripped over Arthur lying on the floor. He'd been shot."

Amanda sat up straighter. "How is he?"

"He'll be fine. He got shot in his upper leg, nothing serious."

"His upper leg? That sounds pretty serious."

Marcie grinned. "His buttocks, actually. I guess he was trying to twist away when Susan turned on him with the gun."

"Poor Arthur, I guess even when he tries to be a hero it doesn't quite work out."

"We have to be fair. If it weren't for him we'd both be dead. He was hiding in the back of the house and heard some of what Susan said. He called the police on his cell phone. It took a while for him to convince them he wasn't pulling a prank, but finally they agreed to send a car out to the inn and alert the volunteer fire department."

"What about Michael Phelps?"

"Arthur saw him coming around the house and jumped him with the tire iron. He managed to knock him out."

"Then he came down to rescue us, and Susan shot him. But how did the two of you escape?"

"I helped him to his feet. I figured I'd help him, then come back for you. We weren't that far from the hatchway stairs. We just kept going forward toward the fresh air."

"But it seemed to me that the door closed."

Marcie nodded. "Apparently Michael Phelps wasn't as knocked out as Arthur thought. We were almost to the top of the stairs when he suddenly appeared and shut the door on us. We tried to push it open, but he used his weight to keep it closed until he could chain it. Guess he didn't care that he was locking Susan in as well. Fortunately it turned out that the door was made of wood and kind of rotted. Arthur had held on to his crowbar, so we used it to break through the door and climb out." Marcie paused and shuddered. "We were both only half conscious toward the end. It was a close thing."

"When did the police and firemen get there?"

"Almost as soon as Arthur and I got out. I wanted to go back in the cellar to look for you, but they wouldn't let me. Otherwise I would have."

Hearing the guilt in Marcie's voice, Amanda reached over and patted her hand.

"I know you would. Did they manage to catch Phelps?"

"He'd already run off. The police are looking for him. They figure he won't get far. After all, he's a local guy, and not the brightest one at that."

"And Susan?" Amanda knew that was someone who would be haunting her nightmares for a long time.

"She didn't make it. A team of firemen went into the cellar and brought her body out while you were being treated on the ambulance."

Amanda leaned back into the pillows. She didn't wish anyone a death like that, but a world without Susan Marston would be a better place.

"So what happened to *you* down there, and how did you ever find that way out?" asked Marcie.

Amanda debated with herself whether to tell Marcie what she thought had happened. It seemed too private to share, but at the same time she needed to tell someone. When Amanda finished her account, Marcie was silent for several seconds.

"I've read that oxygen deprivation can do strange things to the brain. You knew that door to the coal bin was there from the other night, so maybe your mind just used your memories of your father to motivate you across the room to find it."

"I never even noticed where the bin was located when I was down in the cellar."

"Not consciously, but on a deeper level you must have," Marcie replied.

"And that box happening to be under the door so I could climb out?"

"Luck?"

"I suppose."

"Hey, I'm the one who believes in ghosts. Let's not go reversing roles here."

Amanda smiled wanly. "I'm sure that in a few days I'll agree with you, but right now it all seems pretty real. Anyway, I certainly feel like my father saved my life—in more ways than one."

"Yeah, forgiveness is good, isn't it? Whether it was your father forgiving you or you forgiving yourself doesn't really matter."

"I never figured that Susan was in on it," Amanda said a moment later. "She was the one person in town who didn't seem to have anything to gain from what happened at the inn."

"Don't get down on yourself. You'd have figured out her part in it when you talked to Jimmy Racine again."

"Maybe, or maybe he would have stuck to his story. Susan would have been better off putting more trust in her power over boys."

"In one way Susan got part of what she wanted," Marcie said. "I heard the firemen saying that, even though the inn doesn't look bad from the outside, the support beams and most of the floor boards on the first floor were almost completely burned through. It will cost a fortune to get the place back into usable condition. I don't think John Phelps is ever going to see this place used as an inn again."

"Just as well. Four people have died in that basement starting with Charity O'Neil. Even if I don't believe in ghosts, that still strikes me as a bad atmosphere for an inn, don't you think?" Amanda said.

When Marcie didn't respond, Amanda glanced over at her and saw that her friend was staring intently across the room.

"What is it?" Amanda asked.

"Nothing, I suppose. But when the firemen went into the basement to look for Susan, they said that they heard the voice of a girl crying. It couldn't have been Susan. She was already dead. They searched all around but couldn't find anyone else. Finally they figured it must have been some funny sound that the burning building made."

Marcie took a deep breath and hugged herself.

"Pretty weird, huh?"

Amanda nodded. "You know, tomorrow, right after we're done with the police, I think we should head back to the office. What do you think?"

Marcie smiled. "I'm with you, boss. I'm ready to see the ocean again. But let's pay Arthur a visit before we go. We should thank him and let him know the whole story."

"He deserves that," Amanda agreed. "Too bad Professor Wilmot will never know what happened, but I guess telling her son is the next best thing."

"Maybe she does know," Marcie replied.

Amanda looked thoughtful. "Yes, maybe she does."